Volume III

by James Preller

SCHOLASTIC INC.
New York Toronto London Auckland Sydney
Mexico City New Delhi Hong Kong Buenos Aires

Contents

Interior illustrations by Jamie Smith
Cover illustration by R.W. Alley
Book design by Dawn Adelman

12 11 10 9 8 7 6 5 4 3 2 1 5 6 7 8 9 10/0

Printed in the U.S.A. 40

This edition created exclusively for Barnes & Noble, Inc.

2005 Barnes & Noble Books

ISBN 0-7607-9600-9

First compilation printing, December 2005

The Case of the Marshmallow Monster

For my camping buddies, Lisa, Nicholas, and Gavin.
And special thanks to my neighbors, Emily and David,
for teaching me the words to Mila's handclap rhyme.
—J. P.

Chapter One
Closed for Vacation

I hung a sign on my tree house. It read CLOSED FOR VACATION. If someone needed a detective, they'd be out of luck. Because Jigsaw Jones, private eye, was getting away from it all.

Let's face it. Nobody gets rich from detective work. Most kids earn their money by doing chores around the house. The chores aren't fun, and they aren't pretty. Like walking the dog, taking out the garbage, or even making the bed. I mean, why bother making the bed? You're just going to *unmake* it later on.

That's why I became a detective. For a dollar a day, I make problems go away. It's good work. It's honest. You meet interesting people. And you never have to fold sheets.

But like I said, I needed a break.

Too bad I wasn't going to get one. I guess there's always somebody who needs a detective. Even on camping trips.

After all, missing marshmallows are a big problem.

And lake monsters are an even bigger problem. Yeesh.

It started on the first day of our third annual neighborhood camping trip. Every summer a group of fathers organizes it. This year we were going to Enchanted Lake State Campgrounds. My dad said it would be our best trip ever. Twenty-three kids were going, both boys and girls. We'd hike, swim, and play flashlight tag. We'd build roaring fires and sleep in tents. We'd toast marshmallows and eat s'mores until our stomachs hurt. S'mores are a sandwich made of graham crackers, a melted marshmallow, and a piece of chocolate.

Everyone wants to eat some more! That's why we call them s'mores.

Best of all, Shirley Hitchcock's dad

always told us spooky stories around the campfire. He scared us silly, then sent us off to bed. It was fun to lie awake under the stars, listening for creepy sounds in the night.

Oooooh.

Creeeeeeak.

Squish, squish, squish.

Deep down, we knew that Mr. Hitchcock's stories weren't true. There were no such things as forest monsters and bogeymen and killer porcupines.

Right?

Toot-toot. I heard my dad sound the car horn. It was time to leave. I raced to the front of the house. We all piled into the minivan. Mr. Jordan sat beside my dad in the front passenger seat. I sat squished between Joey Pignattano and Ralphie Jordan. My brothers Daniel and Nick were squeezed in the back with all the gear.

And they were complaining already.

"Boys, we're still in the driveway," my dad said. "Could you hold off on the complaints until we get around the block?"

Nick protested, "But I've got a tent pole digging into my ribs!"

Nick was right. I'd seen sardines with more legroom.

"The campground is only two hours away," my dad replied. "You'll live." He put the car into reverse.

My mom waved good-bye from the driveway. "I'll miss you," she called. I wasn't too sure about that. She seemed happy to see us go.

Thrilled, in fact.

Go figure.

Chapter Two

A Tent with Hiccups

We got to the campground right on time. That is, if your idea of "right on time" includes a flat tire and getting lost in the middle of nowhere. That's the place right after my dad says, "I know a little shortcut."

It's a few miles past "I don't need a map."

Naturally, we were the last to arrive at the campground. After another hour, we finished setting up. I was going to share a tent with Ralphie and Joey. My brothers had their own tent.

That's when I noticed the tent beside us. It wasn't a tent, exactly. It was more like a crumpled-up lump on the ground. I looked closer. It was moving.

And muttering.

Oof. Ouch. Hiccup. "What the . . . ?" *Hiccup.* "Heeelp. Er, I'm trapped. Get me outta this thing!"

Joey pointed. "I think it's alive."

"And it's got the hiccups," Ralphie noted.

I poked it with a stick. "Anybody in there?"

A voice answered. "Yes. It's me! Stringbean!" *Hiccup!* "I've been trapped in here for hours!"

Stringbean Noonan, I thought. That was a surprise. I didn't expect to see him here. Stringbean's real name was Jasper. And he wasn't the outdoor type.

"Hold on. Let me find the zipper," Ralphie said. He fumbled around for a moment. Then . . . *ziiiiiiip.*

In a moment, Jasper crawled out, red-faced and sweaty. He kicked the heavy nylon tent. "That thing" — *hiccup!* — "nearly ATE me!"

We all laughed.

Joey discovered that Stringbean had forgotten one very important thing. Tent poles!

Stringbean shrugged. "Don't look at me," he replied. "I don't know anything about camping. I wouldn't even be here if my dad

didn't make me come. I'd rather be eating cheese puffs and watching Nickelodeon!"

Stringbean Noonan was the kind of kid who was afraid of his own shadow. He was afraid of bees, thunder, horses, lightning, and heights.

Now he could add something else to the list.

Tents.

The poor guy was afraid of tents.

Chapter Three

To Build a Fire

Our group had reserved twelve sites in the campground. Right away, the dads turned two sites into the cooking and eating areas. They carried over a bunch of picnic tables and put them in a U-shape. It looked really cool.

There was an open field across the way. Beyond that, a lake with a little sandy beach. We found my dad and Mr. Jordan by the cooking area. They were laughing, unloading food, and putting things in order.

"Who's cooking tonight?" Ralphie asked.

"You're looking at him," my dad said.

Ralphie whispered to me, "I hope your dad is a better cook than driver. I thought we'd never get here."

My dad frowned. "I heard that, Ralphie. Never fear, Chef Jones is here! Spaghetti dinner tonight! I promise not to take a shortcut looking for the meatballs."

We told them about Stringbean's missing tent poles. Mr. Jordan knelt down in front of Stringbean. "Don't worry, Greenbean. We'll find a place for you to sleep."

Jasper mumbled, "It's Stringbean, sir."

Mr. Jordan looked confused. He couldn't understand Stringbean's mumble-jumble. "String cheese?" he asked. "Do you want a piece of string cheese?"

"Never mind," Stringbean said.

My dad spoke up. "You can sleep with Jigsaw's brothers Daniel and Nick. They have extra room in their tent."

Mr. Jordan stood and pointed. "Ah, here comes everybody."

We saw a large group of kids walking toward us from the lake. They were wet and smiling. "You guys missed it!" Mila Yeh cried out. "The lake's awesome. Where have you been?"

Mila was my friend and partner. We did all our detective work together. Mila looked at us, then at my dad. "Don't tell me. Your dad got lost again."

"Lost?" my dad said. "Lost?! I wouldn't call it lost."

Mr. Jordan laughed. "What would you call it, then?"

My dad arched an eyebrow. "The scenic route," he replied. "Anyway, gather some wood, kids. We'll make a bonfire tonight. In the meantime, I'll start cooking."

After dinner, Lucy Hiller's father taught us how to build a "proper" fire. Then he firmly told us we should never, ever build a fire.

I scratched my head and watched.

"You need three kinds of wood for a fire," Mr. Hiller explained. He held out a handful of pine needles, dry grasses, and wood shavings. "This is called tinder. It catches fire easily and burns fast."

He set a small pile in the fire area. "Next, we need kindling. These dry twigs will do nicely." He set them on top of the tinder in a little pyramid.

Mr. Hiller lit the tinder. A few small flames began to lick at the kindling. Mr. Hiller explained, "When the kindling catches, we'll add larger pieces of wood. Dead, dry sticks are best. There seem to be plenty lying around. Go find some, boys and girls. Remember, don't hurt any trees. Leave the living branches alone. I only want deadwood that's already on the ground."

After we gathered wood for the fire, it got

dark. A gang of us played flashlight tag in the field. Then it was story time. Mr. Hitchcock told the coolest, scariest stories. And along with it — we ate s'mores!

It was only the greatest food on the planet.

Chapter Four

Mr. Hitchcock Tells a Story

Mr. Hitchcock wasn't green. And he didn't have a stem growing out of his head. But other than that, he looked exactly like a pear. With arms and legs, naturally. Mr. Hitchcock had narrow shoulders and a wide stomach. His head was large and perfectly bald. His lower lip was thick and he didn't appear to have a neck.

He sat down with a heavy grunt. We all watched him closely. Four-year-old Sally-Ann Simms, who was the youngest kid on the trip, sat on the log between Mr.

Hitchcock and Jasper Noonan. I liked Sally-Ann. She was a hurricane in lavender and pink. If you told Sally-Ann a scary story, she'd just shrug. Then she'd politely request, "More blood, please."

Mr. Hitchcock shivered. He said loudly to no one in particular, "Well, I talked to the ranger. She said everything's been quiet. No signs of the lake creature. So I think we'll be safe."

"Lake creature?" Danika Starling asked.

"Like, whoa. Back up. Did you say lake creature?"

"Oh, never mind," Mr. Hitchcock said. He glanced nervously in the direction of the lake. "It's probably nothing. I doubt the stories are true."

"What stories?" my brother Nick asked.

"Yeah, what stories?" piped up Wingnut O'Brien and his best friend, Freddy Fenderbank. Wingnut and Freddy were like peanut butter and jelly. You never saw one without the other. This was their first time on one of our camping trips.

Wingnut was my next-door neighbor. I didn't know much about Freddy. He had messy red hair and less than a million freckles. From the look of his clothes, I'd say he'd recently been attacked by a mud puddle.

Mr. Hitchcock stirred the fire with a long stick. He shifted uncomfortably in his seat. We sat gathered around the warm flames, waiting. “I shouldn’t have said anything,” he muttered, scolding himself. “I don’t want to scare you kids.”

A chorus of voices went up.

“It’s okay.”

“We won’t get scared.”

“Besides, we like getting scared.”

I noticed Jasper Noonan’s face turning white. He didn’t say a word.

Sally-Ann nodded enthusiastically. “Scare us!” she demanded.

Mr. Hitchcock sighed. “Well, maybe I

should tell you. But only for your safety."

Everyone sat perfectly still, hardly breathing. *WHOOOOOO.* An owl hooted from a distant tree. Mr. Hitchcock gazed into the night sky. A full moon gazed back. He sighed. "It began a few years ago," he said. "It was a misty night like tonight, full of shadows and dark gloom."

Mr. Hitchcock continued, "It's on full moons like tonight, you know, when the creature crawls out of the lake. He slips into the darkness and prowls around."

Chapter Five

Sweet Dreams

"What does the lake creature look like?" Ralphie asked.

"Hard to say," Mr. Hitchcock replied. "Some say it's eight feet tall and covered with scales. Some say it's dark green. Others say it's as black as night. Some say it's got claws. One man swears it's got webbed feet. They say it's afraid of light — fire and flashlights, mostly. But no one has gotten a real good look at the creature. In fact, only one person has seen it up close. And he's not talking anymore."

Danika Starling stood up, waving her arms. “Whoa, whoa, whoa,” she said. “Not talking anymore? Like, you’re not saying that he’s . . .”

“Dead?” offered Mr. Hitchcock. He shook his head. “No, not dead. He’s just *not talking anymore*. To anyone. He just lies in bed and stares at the ceiling. Too scared to even speak.”

"Wh-wh-what happened to him?" Jasper stammered.

Mr. Hitchcock stabbed at the fire with his stick. Orange sparks flew into the sky. "No one knows for sure," he said. "It was late at night. The boy was camping right over there." He pointed. "Well, you know what they say about camping: *Never leave your tent at night without a flashlight.*

"Well, this boy didn't listen. He had to use the bathroom. But he forgot his flashlight. That's probably when he ran into the lake creature." Mr. Hitchcock shook his head sadly. "The poor, poor child."

A chilling cry broke the silence. *Hoooooowl. A-oooooo.* Mr. Hitchcock turned sharply, listening. "Coyotes," he murmured. "Just coyotes."

Then he stood, rubbing his hands together. "Don't worry, kids," he cheerfully announced. "The creature won't bother you. Just keep quiet. Stay in your tents. Everything will be fine."

"Wh-wh-why does it prowl around?" Freddy asked.

Mr. Hitchcock rubbed the top of his bald head. "Food," he whispered. "The creature loves human food."

Freddy gulped.

Mila swallowed hard.

Jasper sneezed.

Nicole wheezed.

And Sally-Ann shouted, “PLEASE! Tell us more!”

Mr. Jordan interrupted the story. “I’d say that’s enough for tonight, Alfred. It’s time these kids got ready for bed.” Mr. Jordan pointed at me and a few others. “Come with me, kids. I’ve got a job for you.”

We followed Mr. Jordan to the cooking area. He lit a kerosene lamp and handed Ralphie a large garbage bag. “I want this area spotless,” he said. “Not a single crumb. Hungry animals live in these woods — including black bears. Leaving food out is an invitation for trouble.”

“Would a bear come into camp?” Mila asked.

Mr. Jordan ran his fingers over his mustache. “If you left food out? Absolutely. They love a free meal. But a raccoon is much more likely. Those little rascals are real scavengers.”

Ralphie chimed in, “That’s why raccoons wear black masks! They steal food!”

Mr. Jordan chuckled. Then he left us alone to clean up.

Danika came up beside me. “Do you believe in the lake creature?” she asked.

I shrugged. “I don’t know. Maybe. It might be true. Like Bigfoot.”

Danika shivered. “To think I went swimming in that lake today. Whoa. That’s, like, *sooooo* not cool.”

Wingnut O’Brien stared at the cleaned-up site. He looked worried. “What if the lake creature comes — and there’s no food?”

“He’ll still be hungry,” Joey said. “For human food.”

“And he’ll want to eat one of us!” Ralphie joked. “Bwaa-ha-ha.”

“Don’t joke around,” Danika scolded. “You’re creeping me out.”

“Let’s leave some food out for it,” suggested Joey. “Just a little snack.”

"No way!" Mila cried. "You heard Mr. Jordan. Food is an invitation for trouble."

We took a vote. Only Mila and Danika voted against it. Sally-Ann grabbed a bag of marshmallows. "The lake creature will love these," she said, handing me the bag.

Mila sighed. "I have a bad feeling about this, Jigsaw. A very bad feeling." Mila felt a little better when we put the bag at the edge of the woods, near a pile of rocks. "At

least now the creature won't wander into the center of camp," she reasoned.

Before zipping up our tent for the night, we saw my father checking the area. He was carrying a garbage bag and a flashlight. He wore a blanket wrapped around his shoulders. "Good night, boys," he called kindly. "Sweet dreams."

Yeah. Sure. Sweet dreams.

Sour nightmares was more like it.

Lake creatures.

Yeesh.

Chapter Six

A Secret Message

"Jigsaw, Ralphie, wake up!"

Morning. Ugh. I tried to lift my eyelids. It might have been easier to lift a piano with my pinkie.

Joey was urgently whispering, "The marshmallows are gone!"

Ralphie snapped awake. "It's real. The lake creature is real!"

Camp was soon buzzing with the news. It's all anyone talked about over pancakes and orange juice. Everybody was scared and excited. The story kept getting bigger and bigger. And now the lake creature had a new name.

The Marshmallow Monster!

After breakfast, I found a note on my sleeping bag.

HOW BARK APE
SEEK SWIM
DIRT SEEN
LIKE EAT
TOOTH A FLOWER
BAT TALK
VERY BIG CAR
BEAR IS BLACK
BUT IS
NOT SLEEPING

The note was from Mila. She always tested my brainpower with secret codes. I inspected the paper. It had been folded twice, leaving heavy crease marks. I noticed that certain letters landed on the creases. I took out a yellow marker and drew a line down the creases.

That's it, I thought. It's a crease code. The trick was to start with folded paper. Then Mila wrote the message in the creases of the paper. None of the other letters mattered.

I quickly figured it out. WE HAVE A NEW CASE.

I found Mila down by the lake. She was sitting across from Danika Starling. They were singing a handclap rhyme.

"Chicka-chicka, boom-boom.
I can do karate!
Chicka-chicka, boom-boom.
I can move my body!
Chicka-chicka, boom-boom.
I won't tell my mommy!
Chicka-chicka, boom-boom.
Oops, I'm sorry!"

At “Oops,” they pushed each other on the forehead and giggled.

“What’s up?” I said.

“Danika wants to hire us,” Mila explained.

I frowned at Danika. Dark rings circled her eyes, like she didn’t get enough sleep last night. I shook my head. “Sorry, closed for vacation. I’m not taking any cases.”

“What do you mean, you’re not taking any cases?” Danika said.

"Just what it sounds like," I replied. "I've been working too hard lately."

Danika's eyes narrowed. "You're afraid, aren't you?"

I answered with a long, slow yawn.

I looked around. It was a perfect day. That is, if you go for blue sky and sunshine. The lake was empty. A lone lifeguard sat staring into space. "How come no one's swimming?" I asked.

Danika put her hands on her hips. "Like, duh. With that lake creature out there? No way anyone's going in that water!"

I nodded. "Why take chances, right?"

"Right," Danika said.

Don't ask why I did what I did. Because I'm not even sure myself. I slipped off my sneakers and socks. I pulled off my shirt. And walked into the lake.

"Jigsaw! What are you doing?!" Mila cried.

"Swimming," I answered. I dove headfirst

into the murky black water. The lake felt cool against my body. I swam out a little farther. Then farther.

"Come back, Jigsaw," Danika urged. "The lake creature!"

I called back, "I'm not afraid of any lake creature."

That's when I felt it.

Something brushed against my leg.

Something slithery.

Like weeds. Or a fish. Or a snake.

Or a . . . *finger.*

I kicked my leg away. My feet strained to touch bottom. They reached, barely. The bottom was gooey, like mud. For a brief moment, my feet felt stuck. Not like mud, I thought. Like quicksand! A wave of fear washed over me.

Then I felt it again.

Something scratching against my skin.

Something was in the lake with me.

Something I couldn't see.

I kicked my legs free and raced for shore. When I reached the beach, I bent over, panting hard.

"Wow, you're a fast swimmer," Danika observed.

I stared at her blankly. "I've changed my mind," I gasped, still puffing hard. "I'll take the case."

No lake creature was going to make a monkey out of me.

Chapter Seven

Piecing the Clues Together

When I need to think, I do jigsaw puzzles. It's like solving mysteries. Each piece is a little clue. All you've got to do is put it together, piece by piece.

Unfortunately, I didn't pack any puzzles for the trip. After all, I was on vacation. I didn't plan on thinking. But I did bring some markers and my detective journal. I never left home without them.

I turned to a clean page and wrote, The Case of the Marshmallow Monster. Beneath that, I wrote, Client: Danika Starling.

Under *Crime* I wrote, *Stolen Marshmallows.*

I wrote the word *Clues*. I underlined it. I chewed on my marker and tried to think. The chewing didn't help get my brain started. It didn't do much for the marker, either. I didn't have a clue. But I did have a suspect. Unfortunately, it lived in the lake and tickled swimmers for laughs.

I drew a picture of the lake creature. It was so good I nearly scared myself.

Ziiiiiip. A noise from behind startled me. Joey Pignattano climbed into the tent. His knee landed hard on my ankle. "Hey, Jigsaw," he asked. "You don't have any ginger ale, do you?"

"No," I replied. "Look in the coolers by the picnic tables. Maybe in there."

Joey turned to leave. This time, he crushed my foot. "Sorry, Jigsaw!" he apologized. "I didn't mean to step on your foot."

"That's okay, Joey. I walk on it, too."

"Huh?" Joey said.

I watched as my little joke sailed over his head, out of the tent, into the clear sky beyond. "Never mind," I grunted. "Why do you want ginger ale, anyway?"

"Wingnut and Freddy have stomachaches. I figured some ginger ale might help them feel better," Joey said.

"Too many s'mores?" I wondered.

Joey made a face. "Too many s'mores? Impossible! There's never enough." Then he left to look for ginger ale. That's Joey for you. Just an all-around nice guy.

I closed my notebook. Mr. Hiller was leading a hike to a nearby waterfall. I

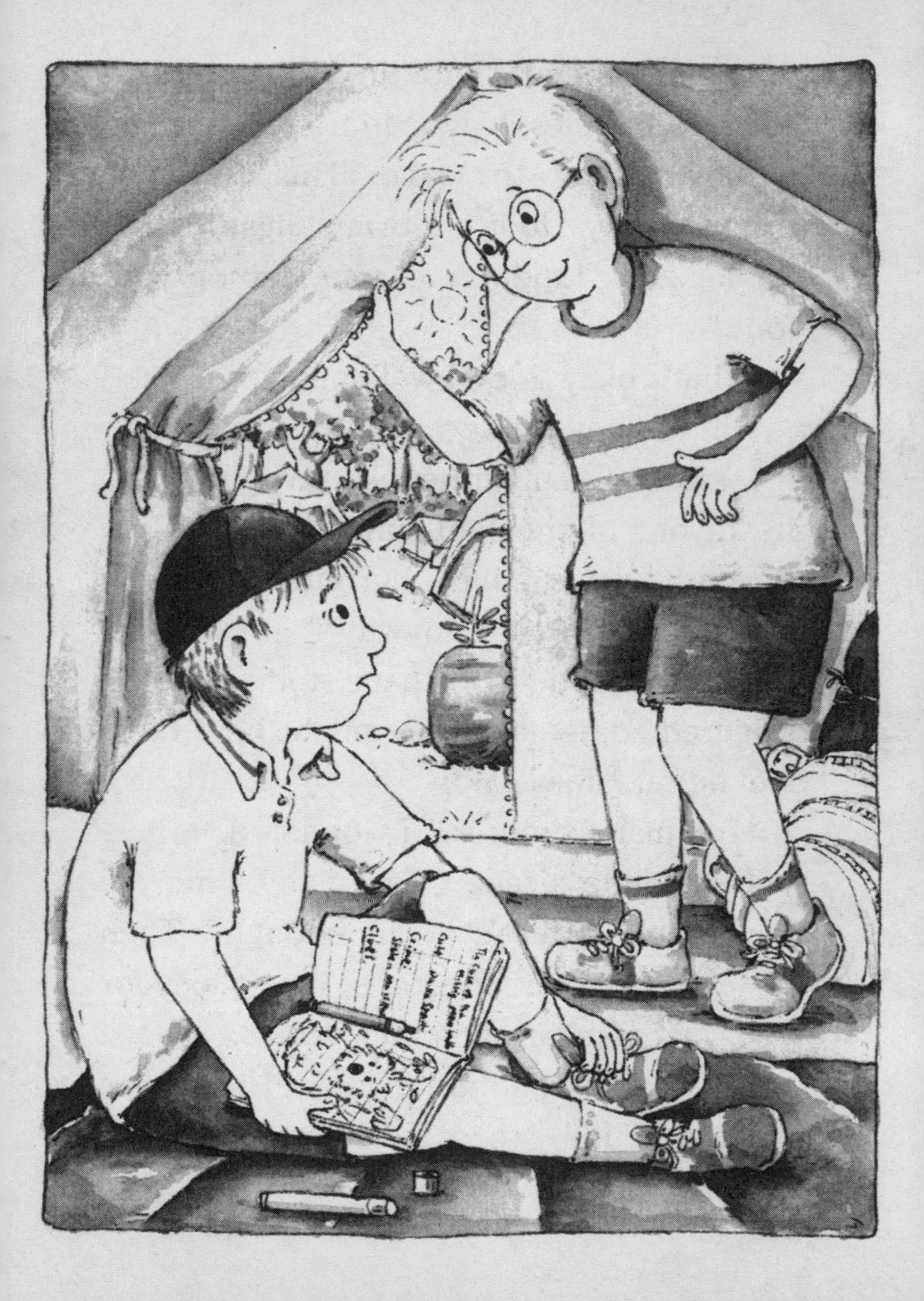

wanted to go. But I had a picture of George Washington in my pocket. His face was on the dollar bill Danika gave me. Someone — *or something* — was stealing marshmallows. George said it was my job to find out who and try to stop him.

Even if it's a monster.

Covered with green slime.

Who prowls in the night.

Next vacation, I promised myself, I'm going to Disney World.

OFFICE

Chapter Eight

More Suspects

"So, this is your office, huh," Mila said.

"That's what the sign says," I replied. I'd spent the last half hour putting a bunch of sticks on the ground. They spelled out O-F-F-I-C-E.

"Some office," Mila teased. "It looks like a big rock to me."

"Hey, give me a break," I said. "It *is* a big rock. You have to use your imagination. Did you find any clues by the lake?"

Mila shook her head. "Nope. No strange footprints. Not a single sign of the lake creature. To tell you the truth," she said, "I'm not convinced it's real."

I thought about my swim in the lake. When I closed my eyes, I could still feel it: that thing scratching at my legs. I showed Mila a page in my journal. "We've got a long list of suspects."

SUSPECTS
★ Lake Creature
★ Black bear
★ Raccoon
★ Squirrel
★ Joey Pignattano
★ Ralphie Jordan
★ Danika Starling
★ Freddy Fenderbank
★ Wingnut O'Brien
★ Sally-Ann Simms
★ Stringbean Noonan

I pointed to the bottom half of the list. "These people were all there when we put out the marshmallows. That makes them suspects."

Mila nodded silently, thinking. She crossed her arms and rocked back and forth. "Danika slept in the tent with me. She never left. It couldn't be her."

I drew a line through Danika's name.

"What about Joey?" I asked. "He had the opportunity."

"But he discovered the missing marshmallows," Mila protested.

"Exactly," I replied. "Joey got up when we were all asleep. He could have eaten the marshmallows, then lied about it."

Mila pulled on her long black hair. She snapped her fingers. "Joey ate six pancakes this morning. That's a lot. He couldn't have eaten a bag of marshmallows, too."

"Are you kidding?" I snorted. "Joey will eat anything, anytime, anywhere. This is

OFFICE

a guy who once ate a worm for a dollar. When it comes to eating, Joey is the Energizer Bunny. He never stops."

Mila nodded. "Okay. He's still a suspect."

I moved further down the list. "Ralphie never left the tent." I crossed out his name.

"Stringbean?" Mila asked.

"Doubt it," I said. "He doesn't like the dark. But I'll check with my brothers to make sure."

That left three names: Sally-Ann, Wingnut, and Freddy.

"Sally-Ann shared a tent with Shirley Hitchcock," Mila said. "I'll see what I can find out."

"I'll talk to Wingnut and Freddy," I said. "But let's check the scene of the crime first. There might be clues."

We walked over together. "I hope it wasn't one of our friends," Mila said. "I hate when that happens."

"Yeah, but it beats having a hungry bear wandering around our camp," I replied.

Mila laughed. "That's it! All we've got to do is find a bear with a stomachache!"

I stopped. "What did you say?"

"It was a joke," Mila explained. "If a bear ate all those marshmallows, he wouldn't be feeling too well."

I remembered Joey's search for ginger ale. I thought about Wingnut and Freddy. And I suddenly had a lot of questions rattling around my head. And each question needed an answer. Just like cookies needed milk.

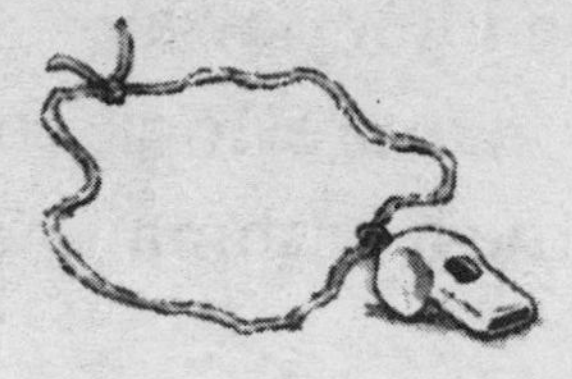

Chapter Nine

The Confession

The scene of the crime was a bust. "It hasn't rained in a while," Mila said, frowning. "The ground is hard. There aren't many tracks."

I examined a patch of dirt. I didn't find any webbed footprints. I did discover some sneaker prints, but that was no big deal. We'd all tramped around there last night.

"There's no empty marshmallow bag," Mila noticed. "That's strange. An animal wouldn't eat plastic. But it wouldn't throw it away, either."

"Maybe it blew away," I suggested. "Maybe the creature took the whole bag. Maybe it ate the marshmallows somewhere else."

Mila's lips tightened. "Maybe," she said.

We decided to split up. Mila went to check on Sally-Ann Simms. I had to find out about Stringbean.

I talked to my brothers. They said that Stringbean spent the night zipped inside his sleeping bag — head and all! Nick shook his head sadly. "He was scared to death, Jigsaw. Stringbean kept mumbling about lake monsters. He said he'd rather be eating cheese puffs and watching Nickelodeon."

"Weird kid," Daniel observed.

No kidding. I crossed Jasper's name off the list. That left Wingnut and Freddy. I found them sitting by the edge of the lake. They were skipping rocks in the water.

"Feeling better?" I asked.

Wingnut shot a look at Freddy. Freddy stared at the ground. Wingnut nervously pulled on his ear. Freddy kicked a rock. "Er, sure," Wingnut stammered. "We feel fine."

Freddy bobbed his head up and down. Like he really, really agreed with Wingnut. It was funny watching them. They weren't very good at lying.

"I heard you guys were sick this morning. What was the matter? Too many marshmallows?"

Wingnut pulled on his ear. Freddy bit his lip. Both stared at the ground.

"Look, guys," I said. "Let's not play games. You took the marshmallows, didn't you?"

"Took the marshmallows?! No way!" Wingnut protested. He looked directly into my eyes. "Honest, Jigsaw. We didn't touch the marshmallows."

I believed him. Wingnut didn't pull on his ear or look away. Instead, his eyes met mine. But something was still wrong. "Explain the stomachaches," I demanded.

Freddy and Wingnut exchanged looks. "We can't," Wingnut said. "We might get into trouble."

That wasn't good enough for me. I wanted facts. And I wasn't leaving without them.

Freddy finally broke down and confessed. "Please don't tell anyone, Jigsaw," he pleaded. "I know we weren't supposed to bring candy into our tents. But . . ."

"Candy?" I repeated.

"Yeah," Wingnut said, smiling at the memory. "A jumbo package of Reese's peanut butter cups. We ate them all!"

"Six each," Freddy said proudly.

"We felt pretty sick," Wingnut admitted. "But it was worth it."

I crossed their names off the list. "Don't worry, guys. I won't say a word."

I was still laughing to myself when I ran into Danika Starling. The afternoon light was fading fast. "Did you find the marshmallow monster?" she asked.

"Tonight," I promised.

Danika's eyes widened. "Tonight? That's, like, *soooo* cool!"

"Yeah, it's like that," I replied.

"So what's your plan?" she asked.

"Night surveillance," I said.

"Surveillance? What's that?" Danika asked.

"It's watching without being seen," I answered.

"Oh, spying," Danika said. "Can I come with you?"

I shook my head. "Too dangerous. It's something I have to do alone."

Danika took off her necklace. She handed it to me. I saw that it was a leather string with a whistle attached. "You might need it," she said. "You know how to whistle, don't you? You just put your lips together and blow."

Chapter Ten

Waiting in the Dark

Shirley Hitchcock said that Sally-Ann Simms snored through the night. We crossed her name off the list. Besides monsters and wild animals, Joey was the last suspect left.

During s'mores, I placed another bag of marshmallows in the same spot as before. I made sure Joey knew about it, too.

The trap was set.

Together, Mila and I picked a spot for me to hide in. It was a few feet past the clearing, into the forest. It was behind a huge oak tree, not far from the marshmallows. I could see the entire campground from there. Hopefully, no one could see me.

I waited until Joey and Ralphie were fast asleep. Then I carefully climbed out of the tent. I slowly, slowly zipped it back up, cringing at the sound. No one woke. I reached into my pocket and took the little bell that I'd borrowed from Sally-Ann Simms. I tied it to the outside zipper.

If Joey left the tent, I'd hear ringing in my

ears. I didn't want to believe that he was the marshmallow monster. But I had to make sure.

Each tent had its own flashlight. I took ours just in case. But I didn't turn it on. I cautiously picked my way through the darkness. Finally I reached the tree. *Hoooooowl. A-oooooo.* I trembled. "Just coyotes," I told myself.

There I sat and waited. Alone in the dark. Because that's what detectives do. We sit. We watch. And we wait. Sooner or later, something happens. It always does.

Only tonight, I was hoping for the opposite. I wanted a nice, quiet evening. A night when nothing happens. I fingered the whistle in my pocket. The air was cool. A slight breeze kicked up. Branches shivered. I watched as the moon, like a cold white eye, looked down upon me.

Night settled around me. And with it, the noises of the night. Crickets chittered.

Branches moaned in the wind. An owl screeched. And then, behind me, I heard small feet scampering to safety.

Fears swirled through my brain. Every sound became a footstep. Every shadow became a monster. I slowly grew tired, so very tired. I had trouble keeping my eyes open. I must have fallen asleep. I dreamed of lake creatures and bears. Raccoons and wolves.

I never heard a sound. I suddenly felt something grab my shoulder. . . .

Shake me . . .

"Huh? What?"

"Jigsaw, Jigsaw! It's me!"

A voice in my dream seemed to be whispering to me from far, far away. . . .

"It's me! Mila."

I gazed wildly into the forest. My eyes struggled to make out the shape hovering beside me. Slowly, I saw the whiteness of her teeth, her eyes.

"You were sleeping," Mila said softly. "I've come to stay with you."

I didn't argue. I was glad for the company.

We sat in silence for five minutes. Ten minutes. Fifteen minutes.

Then a branch snapped. Loud and near.

Crack.

Mila squeezed my arm.

"Shhhh. It's coming this way."

Chapter Eleven

Oops

Crunch, crunch, crunch. Steps in the dirt, kicking stones, crushing leaves.

Then they stopped. Slowly got softer, more distant. The steps were moving away from us.

Tinkle, tinkle.

The bell, faint as a whisper! It came from the other direction. "It's Joey," I whispered to Mila. "He must be up."

But we again heard the footsteps coming closer, closer. I realized that the steps were coming . . . from the lake. I remembered Mr.

Hitchcock's words: *The creature crawls out of the lake . . . and prowls around.*

I aimed the flashlight at the footsteps. But I didn't dare turn it on. Not now, not yet. I wanted to remain hidden in the secret dark.

My eyes darted to the pile of rocks. The marshmallows were untouched. I strained to see my tent through the blur of night. "We should have seen him by now," I whispered to Mila. "Joey must have gone the other way, to the bathroom."

"I hope he took a flashlight," Mila whispered back.

Again Mr. Hitchcock's warning came to my ears. *Never leave your tent without a flashlight.*

No, I thought to myself. No, no, no. I had taken the flashlight. I had it in my hand! That meant Joey was wandering around in the dark.

Alone.

Crunch, crunch, snap.

Not alone, I thought. Worse than alone. Much worse. It was out there. The creature.

"Look!" Mila whispered, her voice filled with fear.

It was a hulking shape. Tall and dark and thick. Walking, stopping, bending, stopping. Lumbering toward us. No, toward the marshmallows.

I squeezed Mila's hand. "Grab a stone," I told her. "Ready?"

I felt her nod — a sharp jerk of the head. She was ready. "One, two, three . . . NOW!"

We jumped up and screamed. We threw stones at the creature's body. I blew the whistle. *Tweeet! Twee-tweeeet!*

"What the . . . ? Ouch! Who threw that? WHO'S OUT THERE?!"

The camp swarmed in chaos. At the scream of the whistle, everyone leaped out of their sleeping bags. Voices shouted,

zippers unzipped. People came running, tripping, fumbling in the dark.

I aimed my flashlight at the creature.

And there stood . . . my father.

Oops.

He was rubbing a small bruise on his arm.

And he was not a happy camper.

It took a while to sort things out. At first, my dad was pretty mad. But after I explained things, he understood. Sort of. In a "still angry" kind of way.

He said that he checked the campground every night, making sure everything was in order. "I make sure there's no food left out accidentally," he said. "That's what happened with your marshmallows last night. I found them."

"You ate them?" Mila asked.

"No, Mila," my dad said. "I picked them up and put them in the car . . . where they belong." He glared at me. But he couldn't

keep it up. Slowly, a broad grin crossed his face. He touched the bruise on his arm.

"Does it hurt?" I asked.

He shook his head. "I'll be fine."

Sally-Ann Simms stomped over. "You mean there's no monster?" she asked.

"No monster," my father answered.

"Bummer!" Sally-Ann stormed back to her tent.

Nick and Daniel were impressed. They looked at my dad's bruise. "Nice aim," they said.

"Hey, where's Stringbean?" I asked.

Nick grinned. "Still in his sleeping bag. I don't think he's ever coming out."

"Nice work, detective." It was Danika, smiling brightly. "Thanks. Now I can go swimming again!"

Well, it wasn't exactly the vacation I had

hoped for. I had wanted peace and quiet. Instead, I got marshmallows and monsters.

But if you ask me, vacations are overrated. I prefer a good mystery any day of the week!

The Case of the Class Clown

For Mary Szczech (whose name I can't type without spraining a finger), with thanks for providing me with a "free pass" to her incredible, creative, happy *classroom. And, of course, thanks to all the children in Ms. Szczech's 1999–2000 classroom:*

Katherine, Leanna, Jesse, Nicholas, Darien, Lily, Christopher, Eliza, Grant, Evan, Jessica, Kathleen, Sasha, Jacob, Connor, Kayla, Jillian, Daniel, Danielle, Brian, Kristen, and Karen.

You guys are awesome!
—J. P.

Chapter One

Slimed

You might say that Athena Lorenzo and I had a friendship right out of a picture book. Only I was a little pig and she was the big bad wolf.

Yeesh.

We sat together in my tree house after school. Actually, I sat. Athena was too mad to sit. Instead she huffed and puffed until steam poured out of her ears. She gritted her teeth. She waved her fists. She stomped her feet until the tree house shook.

"Hey, watch it," I complained. "This tree

house isn't made of bricks, you know. That's the little piggy down the road."

Athena suddenly stopped. She gazed at me through large, round eyes. "Say what? The piggy next door?"

"The Three Little Pigs," I explained. "You know, one little piggy built his house with bricks. One used sticks. And the laziest little piggy used straw." I rapped my knuckles on the tree house. "These walls aren't made of bricks. Get it? I don't care

how much you huff and puff, Athena. Just don't blow my tree house down."

Athena's eyes narrowed. "You're strange," she observed.

"*I'm* strange?" I protested. "That's a laugh. You're the one who's acting crazy." I handed Athena a cup of grape juice. "Drink this. It might calm you down."

I leaned back on my hands and watched Athena slurp the juice. She had dark, round eyes and thick eyebrows. Her hair was a tangle of knots and whirls. I thought about why she was here. And I had to smile. It was going to be one of my *stickiest* cases ever.

After all, it began with green slime.

Squishy, squashy, ooey, gooey slime.

It was my job to find out who left it in Athena's gym sneaker. I'm a detective. For a dollar a day, I make problems go away. And Athena Lorenzo had a problem, all right.

Squish, squash. Slimy socks!

"Stop smiling," Athena barked. "It's not funny."

I bit my lip and tried not to smile. "It is sort of funny," I argued. "I mean, when you put your foot in that sneaker . . . and the slime oozed out . . . and you yelled, 'I'VE BEEN SLIMED!' I've never heard so much laughter in my life!"

Just then my partner, Mila, climbed up the tree house. As usual, she was singing. I recognized the tune. It was one of those golden oldies songs that my father's always playing. But Mila changed the words around:

"Who's that girl just a-climbing up the tree?
Singing do-wah-ditty, ditty-dum, ditty-do!
She's got a new case and she needs a clue.
Singing do-wah-ditty, ditty-dum, ditty-do!"

Mila plopped down beside me, cross-legged. "Did I miss much?"

I jerked my thumb toward Athena. "She was having a cow, that's about it."

"What do you mean, having a cow?" Athena asked.

"A temper tantrum," I explained. "That's your problem, Athena. You've got to lighten up. What's the big deal, anyway? Somebody pulled a prank. Just think of it as an April Fools' joke."

"This is November," Athena moaned.

"So? It came early. Big whoop," I sympathized.

"Yeah," Mila chimed in. "It was just harmless fun, Athena. And you've got to admit it. Everybody thought it was *soooo* funny."

"Not me," Athena shot back. "I think someone has a pretty rotten sense of humor. One minute I'm getting dressed for gym class. The next minute I've got a foot full of slime!"

I smiled at the memory.

"Don't smile," Athena demanded. "It *wasn't* funny. When everybody laughed, I felt embarrassed."

Mila pulled on her long black hair. She nodded. "I see what you mean, Athena. Nobody likes to be laughed at." Mila turned to me. "Let's catch this clown, Jigsaw."

I caught Athena's eye and nodded

toward a glass jar. *Ka-ching, kachink.* She dropped in a handful of change.

I opened my detective journal to a clean page. I grinned. "OK, this shouldn't be so tough. After all, how hard can it be to find a clown? All we've got to do is look for somebody with a red nose and big floppy shoes."

Chapter Two

Eating Socks

"No more jokes," Athena threatened. "Or I'll pour grape juice over your head."

I glared at Athena. This case was five minutes old, and she was already bugging me. "Look, Athena. If you want my help, you have to play by the rules. Rule number one: *No messing with the grape juice.*"

I winked at her. Slowly, the corners of Athena's mouth turned up. "I'm sorry," she apologized. "But it makes me crazy. I can't believe someone put slime in my sneaker."

"I understand," Mila said gently. "Do you

have any idea who might have done this?"

Athena shook her head.

"Is anyone mad at you?"

A shrug. "Nope."

"No idea at all?"

Athena brushed some hair from her face. "No idea," she said.

"Think, Athena," I urged. "Did you notice any clues at all?"

Athena reached into her back pocket. She took out a small piece of brown paper. She laid it on the floor, smoothing it with long, thin fingers. "I found this in my cubby."

The note had one word, in fat letters:

I placed the paper inside a plastic bag. "Our first clue," I noted. "Was there anything with it?"

"No, nothing else."

“How about the socks?” I asked. “Do you still have ’em?”

“They’re in my backpack,” Athena said. “I’m taking them home to be washed. Why?”

“Evidence,” Mila said.

“That’s right,” I agreed. “We’ll need to keep the socks. They might be clues.”

Athena raised an eyebrow. “You want my smelly old gym socks? They’re covered with green slime.”

I held open a plastic bag. I explained, “Mysteries are like jigsaw puzzles. Every piece is important.”

Holding the socks by her fingertips, Athena dropped them in the bag. I began to zip it closed. “Wait,” Mila cried. “Taste the socks first.”

I scoffed. “I am *not* tasting Athena’s socks. You taste ’em.”

To my surprise, Mila leaned forward to sniff the bag. Finally, she dabbed her finger

into a glob of slime. Then she brought it to the tip of her tongue.

And licked.

"Disgusting," Athena complained.

Mila dabbed again. She held her green-tipped finger to my face. "You try it," she offered.

"No, thanks," I replied. "I've already eaten."

Mila sucked on her finger and smiled. "Jell-O," she announced. "Lime Jell-O."

"Really?" I dabbed at the sock and tasted it myself. "Hey, that's pretty good."

Chapter Three

The Raisin Circus

Athena left a few minutes later.

"Let's talk inside," I told Mila. We walked to the house. I held open the back door leading into the kitchen. "I'm worried about something."

"Worried?" Mila asked as she stepped inside. "What are you . . . ?"

Mila stopped cold in her tracks. I almost bumped into her from behind. We stood and gaped at my father. He was sitting at the kitchen table, talking to a pile of raisins. That's right — *talking.* We heard him say, "Listen here, you dried-up grapes. I need you to concentrate."

"Hi, Mr. Jones!" Mila cried. "What are you doing?"

My dad glanced up, with a surprised look on his face. He threw a napkin over the raisins and picked up the newspaper. "Oh, er, hi. I didn't hear you kids come in."

"Were you talking . . . *to the raisins*?" Mila asked.

My dad's cheeks turned pink. "Talking to raisins? Whatever gave you that idea?"

I lifted up the napkin, revealing a handful of raisins. "We heard you," I said.

"Oh — *THOSE RAISINS,*" he exclaimed, snapping his fingers. "We weren't talking, exactly." He shifted in his chair. "Don't you kids have anything to do?"

I shook my head.

"No homework? Dog walked?" he asked.

SPORTS
DAILY NEWS

"Dad," I said. "*Why* were you talking to raisins?!"

My dad looked around the room. He cupped his hand around his mouth and whispered, "I'm *training* them."

"You're what?"

"Training them," he repeated. "You've heard of the flea circus? Well, I'm starting a raisin circus."

I groaned. My dad loved practical jokes. I knew he was up to something. Only I didn't know what.

"A raisin circus?" Mila repeated, as if she hadn't heard correctly.

"That's right," he replied. "Just a few easy tricks. Nothing special."

I pulled Mila by the elbow. "Let's get out of here, Mila. We've got work to do."

Mila yanked her arm away. "Wait, Jigsaw." She eyed my father carefully. "What kind of tricks?"

He sighed. "I'm not sure yet. I'd like to

teach them how to jump," he said. "I figure if Mexican jumping beans can do it, why not raisins?"

"Don't listen to him, Mila," I urged. "It's just another one of his jokes. Let's go downstairs."

My dad winked. "Don't worry, Mila. I'll invite you to the show after I get these bad boys trained."

Mila and I left my father alone at the kitchen table. "Your dad's funny," Mila observed.

"Funny how?" I asked. "Funny ha-ha? Or funny strange?"

Mila shrugged. "Both, I guess."

Oh, brother.

We grabbed a few cookies and went down to my basement. "Okay," Mila said. "What's got you so worried?"

Chapter Four
Phony Bologna

I opened my journal. I wrote:

The Case of the Class Clown.

Mila looked over my shoulder. "That's not a good name. We should call it The Case of the Smelly Socks."

I disagreed. "Think about it, Mila. Putting Jell-O in Athena's sneaker was a joke. Right? So who makes jokes?"

"Jim Carrey," Mila answered.

"Alrighty then!" I replied, doing my best Ace Ventura impression. "But what *type* of person makes jokes?"

Mila paused. "A comedian."

"Right," I said. "Or a clown."

"So."

"So," I said. "Who's the class clown in room 201?"

"That's easy," Mila answered. "Ralphie Jordan. He's always messing around."

"Exactly," I said. "It's got to be him. But I can't rat on Ralphie. He's one of my best friends."

Mila thought it over. "We're detectives, Jigsaw. Athena hired us to solve the mystery. We've got to catch the prankster — no matter *who* it is."

Mila was right. She knew it. I knew it. But I didn't have to like it. Not one bit. After all, who wants to be a tattletale? Not Jigsaw Jones, that's for sure.

"Don't worry, Jigsaw. We're not even sure it's Ralphie. It could be anybody."

"Could be," I said, doubtfully.

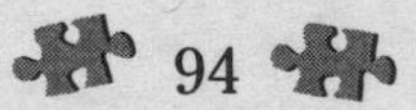

JIGSAW JONES
PRIVATE EYE
$1.00
in
advance

Mila looked at me firmly. "You'll do the right thing."

"That's what worries me," I muttered.

Suddenly my father's voice boomed down the stairs. "Mila! Your stepmother, Alice, just called. She wants you home right now. You're late for a piano lesson."

"Oh, my gosh!" Mila exclaimed, jumping to her feet. "I've gotta go, Jigsaw. See you in school tomorrow!"

Later that night, I got a phone call from Joey Pignattano. He was all worked up. "I need a detective, Jigsaw. It's an emergency! Somebody's out to get me!"

"Slow down," I said. "Take a deep breath and tell me all about it."

"I was almost poisoned!" Joey said.

"Poisoned?!"

"Yeah — *to death*! It happened at school today. In the cafeteria. I took a bite out of my bologna sandwich and tasted something *strange*."

"That's what you get for eating bologna," I said. "They don't call it mystery meat for nothing."

"Stop joking," Joey objected. "This is serious. When I opened my sandwich, I found out that somebody had put in rubber bologna!"

"Rubber bologna?"

"Yeah," Joey said. "Phony bologna."

I'd seen the stuff before. You could buy

it at The Party Store in the Jokes and Gags section. It was right next to the fake throw-up.

"Any other clues?" I asked.

"Yeah," Joey said. "I found a brown piece of paper inside my lunch box. There was writing on it —"

I interrupted him. "Let me guess. It said, 'Gotcha!' "

Joey was impressed. "Wow, how'd *you* know?"

I yawned. “I’m a detective, Joey. Trouble is my business.”

That night, I took a long, hot bath. I lay perfectly still, thinking about my good pal Ralphie Jordan. It sounded like the kind of pranks he’d pull. I put my head under the water and counted as high as I could. When I came up for air, I knew two things: Catching Ralphie wouldn’t be easy. And it wouldn’t be fun.

Some days, being a detective was the toughest job in town. I ducked my head under the water again. For some reason, I liked things better down there.

Chapter Five

Two Lies

The next morning, Mila and I slid into our bus seats. I told her about Joey's call.

"Do you really think it's Ralphie?" Mila asked.

"Probably," I replied. "But whoever did this had to get into Athena's gym bag and Joey's lunch box — without anyone seeing."

Mila rocked back and forth, thinking. "The cubbies!" she exclaimed. "That's where our gym clothes and lunch boxes are stored."

In Ms. Gleason's class, everybody had different jobs. One of the jobs was keeping the cubbies neat. I told Mila, "Find out who was on cubby patrol this week. Maybe they saw something."

Mila nodded. "You got it, Jigsaw."

Ralphie Jordan suddenly popped his head up from the seat in front of us. "Hey, guys! What are you talking about?"

My heart skipped a beat.

Mila stammered, "Er, uh . . . well . . ."

"Homework!" I lied, a little too loudly. "We were talking about homework."

I felt guilty about lying to Ralphie — as if I'd just drowned his pet goldfish.

"Bah, homework!" Ralphie said, making a face. "Forget that! Let's talk about Athena. Wasn't it awesome when she put her foot in that slime? I nearly died laughing."

I didn't feel right hanging around with Ralphie. I was a detective — and he was my number one suspect. It wasn't time to pal around. Just then, the bus pulled up in front of school. I grabbed my pack and hustled off. I was feeling worse than ever. Ralphie was one of my best friends. But now I couldn't look him in the eye.

I was almost glad when Helen Zuckerman cornered me on the way to class. Lately, Helen had been acting a little weird. I mean, even *weirder* than usual. She had been reading a lot of joke books. Then she told corny jokes all day.

Here's the thing. For some reason, Helen Zuckerman had decided to *become* funny. Which is sort of like deciding to become a tall redhead. Some things you just *can't change*. And Helen Zuckerman, no matter how hard she tried, was about as funny as a spelling test.

"Hey, Jigsaw. Why do ghosts hear so well?"

I shrugged.

"Because they're eerie!" Helen snorted and burst out laughing.

I groaned.

"Get it?" she said. "*Eerie?* Like, you know, ears!"

I told her I got it.

"Here's another one," she said.

I started to walk away.

Helen grabbed me by the shoulder. "What kind of books do skunks read?"

"Dunno," I said.

"Best-*smellers*!" Helen howled.

What a stinker. I forced myself to smile.

Helen frowned. "You don't think I'm funny, do you?" Her lower lip trembled. Her face twitched. I could see she was upset.

"Well," I began, "it's just that . . ."

Helen looked at me hopefully.

I couldn't tell her the truth. It would hurt her feelings too much. I finally said, "The

Top Jokes

thing is . . . I heard that joke before. Maybe I'd laugh if you told me another one."

"Really?" Helen asked. "OK. Why did the principal . . . whoops, I messed that up. Sorry! Why did the *vampire* get sent to the principal's office?"

"I give up."

"He had a bat attitude! Get it — *bat* attitude! Like, *bad* attitude. But it's *bat* attitude!"

I could have won an award for best actor. I giggled. I snickered. I snorted. I laughed until my throat hurt. "Bwwwaaaa-haaaa-haaaa!" I screamed. "That's *sooooo* funny!"

Sure, it was a lie. But at least it made Helen smile. I guess lying is OK sometimes. I think. Maybe.

Chapter Six

Drop Everything and Laugh

Ms. Gleason clapped her hands softly, *clap – clap.* That was our signal to be quiet. We all clapped back, *CLAP – CLAP – CLAP.*

Ms. Gleason smiled. "Good morning, boys and girls. I love it when you listen for my signals."

She wiped her hand across her forehead. "Wow, what a morning! My crazy basset hound, Brutus, got loose again. You should have seen me. I was in my bathrobe, chasing Brutus through my neighbor's garden!"

We all laughed. We loved it when Ms. Gleason told us her Brutus stories. Her dog sounded like a real nut. One time, Brutus even ate Ms. Gleason's new shoes!

We began each day by reading our daily letter aloud. Every morning, Ms. Gleason wrote a letter and put a copy on all our desks. At 10:30, we were going to meet with our fifth-grade buddies. In the afternoon, Eddie Becker's grandmother was coming in to read us a story.

Ms. Gleason said, "Meeting Eddie's grandmother will be a lot of fun. I know you will be a polite audience. Remember, pay attention, listen carefully, and be *observant.* You'll write about the story in your journals when she leaves."

For language arts, Ms. Gleason needed help fixing some sentences that were broken. She called me up to the easel. There were two sentences written on it:

that boy don't go to
pottsford school any more

ms willard will learn us how to
multiply this year said irving

It was my job to put in the right punctuation and correct the mistakes. No biggie. Ms. Gleason let me call on other students for help. I liked that. It made me feel like a teacher. I called on Danika

Starling first. She knew the right answer to everything.

In no time at all, we made the sentences as good as new.

~~that~~ That boy ~~don't~~ doesn't go to

~~pottsford~~ Pottsford ~~school~~ School ~~any more~~ anymore.

~~"Ms willard~~ "Ms. Willard will ~~learn~~ teach us how to

multiply this ~~year~~ year," said ~~irving~~ Irving.

After that, we had DEAR time. That's when we had to Drop Everything And Read. We weren't supposed to *drop* anything, actually. But that didn't stop Ralphie Jordan. Every day at DEAR time, he threw something on the ground and hollered, "Look out below!"

We usually laughed. Only this time he dropped a heavy book on Geetha Nair's toe. So it wasn't funny. Geetha was furious. She scolded Ralphie, "You should never mess around with somebody else's toes."

And I guess that made sense.

Sort of. In a weird way.

At lunch, Mila came up to me. "Bad news," she said. "I checked the bulletin

board. Ralphie is on Cubby Patrol this week."

"What about the handwriting?" I asked Mila. "Did you compare the notes to Ralphie's handwriting?"

Mila shrugged. "It's not the same, but that doesn't mean anything. The notes were written in a special way. Nobody writes in fat letters all the time. It would take forever."

I nodded glumly. "This case just keeps getting worse and worse. Look what's for dessert this week." I pointed to my lunch tray. On a small plate sat a shivering pile of lime Jell-O.

I didn't much feel like eating it.

Go figure.

Chapter Seven

The Fish Tank Prank

There were two more pranks on Thursday. I was standing right there when the first one happened. It was a whopper. Mila nearly jumped out of her socks.

When we start the day, we come into the classroom in dribs and drabs. Ms. Gleason's usually out in the hall, chatting with some kids or another teacher. We talk to one another, put our backpacks away, mess around. Until the bell rings, we're pretty much free to do what we want.

"Hey, what's this?" Mila said, surprised.

There was a small round tin on her desk. It had a bow on it. "A present? It's not my birthday."

Mila picked it up. She began to twist it open . . .

I suddenly got a bad feeling. "Wait!" I shouted.

Too late. Another twist and — *sploing!* — some springy snakes shot out of the can and sprang into the air. "ACK!" Mila screamed, nearly falling over a chair.

"Bwaaaa-haaaa-ha, haaa-haaa!" Everyone who saw it laughed. Mila bent down to pick up a piece of brown paper that popped out of the can. She read it, grumbled, and shoved it in her desk.

In the confusion, Athena came up to me. "Any suspects?" she asked.

I glanced around the classroom. My eyes landed on Ralphie, who was laughing hysterically with Eddie Becker.

"Nope," I said coldly.

"None?" Athena asked, eyes wide. "Not one suspect?!"

"Nope!" I snapped. "Not one."

"I thought you were some kind of great detective," Athena growled. "What's the matter? Is this case too hard for you?"

I wiggled two fingers in the air. "Rule number two: *No bugging the detective*."

I walked away without looking back. This prankster was starting to get on my nerves.

Out on the playground, Mila tried to

cheer me up. "Don't worry, Jigsaw. It was just a joke. I'm not mad or anything. It's no big deal, really."

I forced a smile. "Sure. *No big deal.* That's probably what the turkeys said about the first Thanksgiving."

When we got back from afternoon recess, Bigs Maloney was the first person to notice it. From the doorway, he pointed at the fish tank. "LOOK! The water's PINK!"

And it sure was.

Pink as cotton candy.

Not that our goldfish — Elmer, Bugs, and Daffy — seemed to mind. They just happily swam around, *glub, glub, glub.* Goldfish are like that. They don't care whether they live in an Olympic-size swimming pool or a toilet bowl.

Everybody was excited and alarmed. Well, not everybody. I thought Nicole Rodriguez was going to cry. She was a real animal lover. "The poor little fish," she kept saying. "The poor little fish."

"Chill out," snapped Bobby Solofsky. "It's probably just food coloring. I put it on my Rice Krispies all the time."

Lucy Hiller found a note taped to the side of the tank. It was the same brown paper. The same balloonlike letters. The same message: GOTCHA!

"Boys, girls, sit down!" Ms. Gleason ordered. You could tell from her voice that she meant business. Ms. Gleason took the

GOTCHA!

note from Lucy. "Who wrote this?" she asked, looking around the room. "I'm waiting. Who wrote this?"

No one answered. Just nervous coughs and shuffling feet.

Ms. Gleason sat behind her desk. She ran her hand through her hair. "Well, I'm very upset. First, I'm going to see what I can do about this fish tank. I certainly hope that Bugs, Daffy, and Elmer are all right. As for the rest of you, take out your math booklets. I don't want to hear another sound for the rest of the day."

"But . . ." Helen started to say.

"Not a peep," said Ms. Gleason.

Chapter Eight

Dad's Amazing Raisins

We were pretty quiet on the bus ride home. Whenever Ms. Gleason was upset, we always felt worse.

"Oh, yeah, I almost forgot," I grumbled to Mila as we climbed off the bus. "My dad says he's taught the raisins a trick."

Mila snapped her head around. "What?! Is he serious?!"

I lifted my shoulders and let them droop. "You know my dad. He's never serious. It's probably some kind of magic trick. Come over after dinner," I told her. "We need to work on the case, anyway."

After dessert, my father cleared the table. We gathered around — Mom, Grams, Hillary, Daniel, Nick, Mila, and me. Even my dog, Rags, seemed interested. Though I think he was still hoping for scraps. Only my oldest brother, Billy, got up to leave.

"Don't you want to stay to see the swimming raisins?" my dad asked.

Billy waved his hand. "Thanks, but no thanks. But teach 'em how to fly on a tiny trapeze, and I'll pay money to see it."

"It's a deal," my dad answered, chuckling. He took out a bowl of raisins. Then he made a big show out of picking what he called "his five best swimmers."

He poured a large glass of seltzer. "And now, ladies and germs," he announced in a deep voice, "the amazing, terrific, fantabulous, swimming raisins!"

Hillary stifled a yawn.

My dad ignored her. He tossed the

raisins into the glass. "Come on, boys," he commanded. "Swim to Papa!"

Blub, blub, plop. Each raisin floated for a moment, then sank to the bottom.

"That's it?" Nick asked. "That's the trick? You taught them how to drown?"

My dad held up a hand. "Wait . . ."

One by one, the raisins stirred. Slowly, they rolled and jiggled and, finally, "swam"

back to the top of the glass. Then down again, then up, then down, and up again!

My dad stood and bowed. We all laughed and cheered.

"Those *are* amazing raisins," Mila said.

"It's the soda water," Daniel scoffed. "The bubbles make it work."

Mila didn't care. "I can't wait to try this at my house!" she exclaimed.

Chapter Nine

An Unexpected Twist

Mila and I went into my bedroom. I opened my detective journal. It read:

THE CRIMES

1. Green Jell-O in sneakers.
2. Rubber bologna in Joey's sandwich.
3. Tin of snakes for Mila.
4. Food coloring in fish tank.

I turned the page and showed Mila a picture I'd drawn. It was titled "**GOTCHA!**"

Mila frowned. "That doesn't look like me. It's more like the Bride of Frankenstein."

"You should have seen yourself when the snakes popped out," I said. "You *looked* like the Bride of Frankenstein!"

I walked around the room stiffly, with my arms outstretched, like Frankenstein's monster. We both cracked up. That's the thing about pranks. Sooner or later, they usually got a laugh.

"Do you still think it's Ralphie?" Mila asked.

I nodded. I ticked off the reasons on my fingers. "First, Ralphie is always joking. Second, you heard him on the bus. He's the one who's been laughing the loudest at all the pranks. Third, he had *opportunity.* He was on Cubby Patrol this week. I'm almost positive it's him."

"What do we do now?" Mila asked.

"We wait," I said.

"Wait?"

"Yeah," I said. "Ralphie should be over any minute."

"What?!" Mila screeched. "He's coming here? Now?"

I told Mila about my little plan. I gave her a piece of paper. We wrote our names in fat, round letters. Like this:

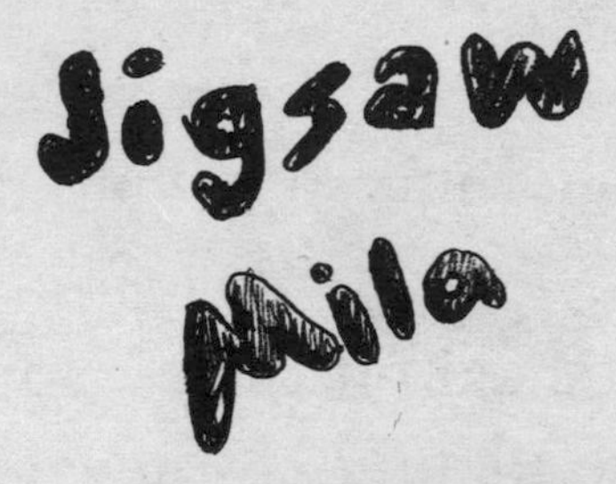

"We'll act like we're having a lot of fun," I told Mila. "Then we'll ask Ralphie to try it."

"Smart," Mila said, nodding. "We might get a match with the 'Gotcha' notes."

Rags barked at the front door. Then I heard my mother's voice. "You know the way, Ralphie. They're in the bedroom."

"Hey, guys," Ralphie greeted us. "What's going on?"

"We're writing our names in fat, round letters!" I announced. "It's so much fun! Try it!"

Mila eagerly shoved a paper and marker into Ralphie's hands.

Ralphie rolled his eyes. "Boring," he groaned. "Let's play Monopoly Junior instead."

Oh, well. It was time for Plan B. I took the direct approach. "I have to ask you a question, Ralphie. Are you the one playing all those pranks?"

Ralphie smiled nervously. A confused expression crossed his face. He looked at Mila, then back at me. "Are you *serious*?"

Our faces told him the answer.

"No way, Jigsaw! It's not me," he said.

"Do you promise?" I asked.

Ralphie promised.

"What about Cubby Patrol?" Mila wondered. "You were the only person who could have done some of those pranks."

Ralphie protested. "I wasn't on Cubby Patrol this week."

Mila raised an eyebrow. "You were listed on the board, Ralphie. I saw it."

Ralphie smiled. "Oh, that. I traded jobs with somebody. I got to clap the erasers instead."

"What?!" Mila and I said together.

"Yeah," Ralphie said, cracking a smile. "It was weird. Helen asked me if I'd switch jobs this week. I was, like, 'Sure!' Anybody would rather clap erasers than straighten up the cubbies."

"Helen Zuckerman," I murmured. "Go figure." I slid my eyes toward Mila. She looked so surprised, you could have knocked her down with a feather.

Ralphie explained, "Helen said she was allergic to chalk dust."

I stretched out my hand to Ralphie. "I want to apologize," I said. "I'm sorry I suspected you."

Ralphie waved the thought away. He couldn't care less. "Sorry? Are you kidding me? I *wish* I'd thought of that stuff. Pink food coloring in the fish tank — that's genius!"

I knew tomorrow would be a busy day. After Mila and Ralphie headed out, I got to bed nice and early. As usual, my dad read with me before tucking me in. We were in the middle of *Shiloh,* by Phyllis Reynolds Naylor. It was a really good story.

My dad closed the book and stood up to leave.

Shiloh

"Hey, Dad . . ."

"Yeah?"

"You were funny tonight, with the raisins."

He looked at me suspiciously. "Funny how?" he asked, rubbing his chin. "Funny strange? Or funny ha-ha?"

I smiled. "Just plain funny."

"Thanks, kiddo," he said, leaning down to kiss me. "I try."

Chapter Ten

In the Library

The next morning Mila and I talked it over at the bus stop. “Helen is the *last* person I would have suspected,” Mila said.

“Tell me about it,” I agreed. “I didn’t think her skeleton *had* a funny bone. But we’re a long way from catching her. We still need proof.”

But getting proof wasn’t going to be easy. All morning, I tried to find witnesses. I talked to so many kids my ears hurt.

No luck.

I even sneaked a peek at Helen’s writing

folder. I was hoping to find a match with the "Gotcha" notes.

It was no luck all over again.

Poor Mila had it even worse. It was her job to hang around with Helen. Ask her tough questions. See if Mila could trick Helen into confessing. Instead, Helen just told Mila bad jokes all day.

By afternoon recess, we were pretty disappointed. Maybe it wasn't Helen after all.

Mila kicked a rock thoughtfully.

"Hey, wait a minute!" I exclaimed. "You know how Helen has been telling all those jokes lately?"

"Nonstop," Mila said, rolling her eyes. "Each one is worse than the next. She's been taking a lot of joke books out of the library."

"The library!" I exclaimed, "What if she read about *practical jokes,* too? I mean, let's face it. Helen's not funny. She has to get her ideas from somewhere."

"Yeah, so?" said Mila.

"So," I said, "follow me."

Ms. Gleason gave us permission to go to the library instead of taking recess.

The school librarian, Mrs. Kranepool, was a large, friendly lady. She wore her hair in a big lump at the top of her head. There were always a few pencils sticking out of it. "May I help you?" she asked kindly.

I told her we were working on a case.

Mrs. Kranepool slid her pointy glasses

down her nose. She peered over them. "A case? Is it very, very dangerous?"

"We just need information," I assured her.

"You've come to the right place," she answered. "Information is our specialty. Do you need help finding a book?"

"Um, not exactly." I pulled out my notebook. "Could you tell us what books Helen Zuckerman has taken out recently?"

Mrs. Kranepool's lips went tight. "Oh, dear," she said. "I'm afraid I can't do that."

"You mean, you don't know?" I was surprised. I thought librarians knew everything.

"It's not that," she replied. "But I'm afraid it's private information. That's Helen's business, not yours. I'm sure you understand."

I didn't. I told her that it was different for detectives. Other people's business *was* my business.

"I'm sorry, I can't help you," Mrs. Kranepool repeated. She began to type away at the computer.

Rats. We struck out.

Suddenly, Mila spoke up. "In that case, do you have any books on practical jokes?"

Mrs. Kranepool glanced at Mila. She pulled a pencil from her hair and tapped it against her open palm. "Practical jokes, hmmmm," she mused. "I seem to remember something. Try the humor section."

We tried. And we hit a grand slam. I pulled a book off the shelf: *Gross Gags and Practical Jokes,* by R. U. Nurvice.

In her excitement, Mila grabbed the book out of my hands, but it fell to the carpet. A paper slipped out of it. "Hey, somebody left a bookmark," Mila noticed. Then her eyes widened. "Look, Jigsaw."

She handed me the bookmark. There

were initials on it written in fat, balloonlike letters: H.Z.

"H.Z.!" I exclaimed. "Those are Helen's initials. She must have left this bookmark in here by accident."

"And check out the lettering," Mila observed. She pulled a piece of paper from her pocket. It read GOTCHA! in the same kind of lettering. The handwriting matched.

Mila flipped through the book. "Listen to this," she said, reading aloud.

> There's nothing funnier than slime. Can't find any slime? Don't worry. Green Jell-O works just as well. When your friend isn't looking, place a hefty scoop of Jell-O in his or her shoe!

Mila turned a few more pages. She read again:

> Food coloring is perfect for playing pranks. Take a wacky color and pour a few drops in your friend's milk. You can even put some in a fish tank! Don't worry, you won't hurt the fish. But you will get laughs from all your pals!

"These are the exact same pranks that happened in school," she said. "This means that . . ."

". . . we finally have our proof!" I said triumphantly.

Mila grinned. "I think it's time we gave Helen a taste of her own medicine."

Chapter Eleven

Gotcha!

Mila and I prepared a message in invisible ink. It was easy enough to do. We wrote the message by using a brush dipped in lemon juice. Then we told Athena what to do. The plan was set.

On Saturday afternoon, right on time, Helen Zuckerman came over to Athena's house. Athena led her into the playroom. Meanwhile, Mila, Joey, and I hid in a nearby closet. We left the door open a tiny crack and watched.

"So what's the big excitement?" Helen wondered.

Athena shoved a paper in front of Helen. "I found this secret message from Mila to Jigsaw," she said. "I bet it's about the case they're working on."

Helen looked sharply at Athena. "What case?"

"The practical joker," Athena said. "Jigsaw says they are hot on the trail."

Helen eyed the paper. "It's blank," she said. "There's nothing on it."

Athena shook her head. "That's because they used invisible ink. But I know how to read it."

Athena brought out a glass jar. She explained, "My mom helped me. It's just water mixed with a few drops of iodine." She handed Helen a small paintbrush. "You just brush it on, and the message magically appears."

Mila giggled quietly.

I poked her in the ribs. “Shhhh.”

We could see that Helen was desperate to figure out what to do. Just as planned, Athena spoke up. “I’ve got to go to the bathroom,” she said. “I’ll be back in a few minutes.”

Athena left Helen alone with the message.

We could see that Helen was worried. She didn’t want to get caught. So of course she

couldn't read the message with Athena in the room. Quickly, Helen painted the iodine mixture on the page. The iodine turned the paper purple. The message written with lemon appeared in white. It read:

Helen's face turned white.

She was caught, and she knew it.

This time, Mila couldn't help herself. She laughed out loud. A booming, rolling, rib-tickling laugh. The next minute, we all spilled into the room — laughing, pointing, and slapping one another on the back.

"Now *that's* funny!" I howled.

Helen frowned. Then slowly, as she watched our happy faces, she smiled, too. "I guess the joke's on me," she said.

There was one last detail. I put my hand

Gotcha Back!

on Helen's shoulder. "I won't tell Ms. Gleason on you," I said. "Because I think it's something you should do yourself."

Helen nodded. "I already did," she confessed. "On Friday."

"Wow," Mila said. "That took guts. Was she mad?"

Helen tilted her head from side to side. "Not really. Ms. Gleason said she was glad that I was honest and told the truth. But she still gave me extra homework. I had to write out all the class rules — five times each!"

Helen glanced back at the paper. She looked at me. "I guess I deserved it," she admitted.

"Just one more thing," Mila said. "Why did you do it?"

Helen made a face. "I guess I wanted to be funny."

I didn't understand.

Helen continued, "Look at Ralphie. He's the most popular kid in class because he makes everyone laugh. I wanted to be popular, too."

"Helen, you don't have to be funny to make friends," Athena said. "You just have to be nice. And you're one of the nicest people I've ever met."

Helen's eyes beamed like two flashlights. Her smile filled the room. "Really?"

"Really," we all answered.

And that was that.

In a few minutes, Athena's mom came into the room. She was carrying a plate of brownies. Like magic, they vanished in a matter of minutes.

Me? I felt great, like I always did after solving a tough case. It took some work, and a lot of help from Mila. But I couldn't wait for the next case. After all, I loved mysteries.

And that's no joke.

The Case of the Detective in Disguise

For Dawn Adelman, Maria Barbo, and Bonnie Cutler. With thanks and appreciation for your hard work, skill, and commitment. I couldn't possibly do it without you.

Chapter One

A Detective Without a Mystery

It was January. And it hadn't snowed all winter.

If you ask me, that's just *wrong*. Because a winter without snow is like a detective without a mystery. Come to think of it, I was like a detective without a mystery. My piggy bank was starving. I had no money to feed it.

My partner, Mila, and I sat in my basement office. I was on my third glass of grape juice when Mila rose to her feet. "We can't sit around all day," she snapped. "We've got to do something."

Mila walked over to our secret hiding place behind the washing machine. She came back carrying a cardboard box. It was labeled:

KEEP OUT AND THAT MEANS YOU!

Mila spilled our box of detective supplies onto the floor. Together, we'd collected some pretty cool stuff. We had walkie-talkies and decoder rings. We had fingerprint kits and how-to books. And we had wigs, clothes, and makeup for disguises.

"Hey, I remember this!" Mila exclaimed. She put a curly green wig on her head. I laughed.

For the next half hour, Mila and I tried on different disguises. Some of them weren't too bad. With a top hat and a hoola hoop, I

KEEP OUT
AND THAT
MEANS YOU!

disguised myself as a lion tamer. I even used Rags as a lion and pretended the hoola hoop was a ring of fire. Only Rags wasn't very good at it. He kept licking the hoola hoop instead of jumping through it. Yeesh.

Mila put on a baseball uniform and a catcher's glove. She tucked her hair under a cap. "I'm Mike Piazza!" She laughed.

My mom came down the stairs, carrying a laundry basket. "Oh, how cute! You're playing dress-up!"

"MOM!" I protested. "This isn't dress-up. It's detective work. We're in disguise."

My mom ran her hand through my hair. "I wanted to remind you that I'm volunteering at the children's hospital this week. I arranged for you to stay at Mike and Mary's after school."

"Yeah, sure, fine," I mumbled. Mike and Mary were old family friends who ran a little sandwich shop near school. It was

called Our Daily Bread and Pita. Clever, huh? I liked going there. But at the same time, I wished I didn't have to be baby-sat. It was embarrassing.

I suddenly had a terrific idea. "A lot of people go into that shop," I told Mila. "If we put up a poster, we'll get some business."

"Great idea, Jigsaw!" Mila exclaimed.

We grabbed some poster board, cracked open a new set of markers, and got to work. Mila was in charge of the fancy lettering. I drew the picture.

"What do you think?" I asked Mila.

She whistled softly. "You're definitely an artist, Jigsaw. But tell me. Is my nose really that big?"

Chapter Two

My Fifth-Grade Buddy

On Monday morning, at 9:14, I was rubbing sleep from my eyes. Mila and I were about to step inside the school when I heard my name.

"Hey, Jigsaw. Think fast!" A football flew toward me. I pretended it was a cold and caught it.

Ben Ewing walked over, smiling happily. "How do you like my new pigskin? It's autographed by Peyton Manning."

"Awesome," Mila said. "He's one of the top quarterbacks in the NFL!"

Ben grinned proudly. He stretched a hand out to Mila. "You're Mila, right? Jigsaw told me about your detective business. My name's Ben."

Mila blushed shyly. "Can I see your football?"

"Sure," Ben replied. "My father bought it on the Internet. It was a present for my eleventh birthday. I brought it in to show my teacher, Mr. Alonzo."

Ben Ewing was my fifth-grade buddy. In our school, all the younger kids were teamed up with "buddies" from the fifth grade. We worked with our buddies on special projects. I was lucky to have Ben as my buddy. It was like having an extra big brother . . . without the painful wedgies.

"Catch any crooks lately?" Ben asked.

I pulled the poster from my backpack and showed it to Ben. "Business stinks," I admitted. "But I think this will help."

Ben was reading the poster when Bobby Solofsky walked up. Bobby lived next door to Ben.

"Hi, Ben!" Bobby said.

"Oh, hi, Bobby," Ben murmured without looking away from the poster.

"I saw you playing catch yesterday!" Bobby said.

"Not now," Ben said. "I'm reading."

Bobby glanced at the poster. He made a sucking sound with his teeth. "Big whoop-de-do," Bobby sneered. "Anybody can be a detective. Besides, his name isn't Jigsaw. It's *Theodore*."

Ben looked annoyed at Bobby. "I don't see *you* solving any mysteries."

Bobby didn't have much to say after that. He just stood quietly, looking down at his shoelaces.

Ben handed back the poster. "Very cool. But I've gotta run. Catch you on the rebound." Ben tucked the football under his arm and took off like a running back.

"Bye, Ben! See you around, pal!" Bobby shouted.

But Ben was long gone.

Chapter Three

Mike and Mary's

I walked home after school instead of taking the bus. That's because I wasn't going home at all. I was headed to Our Daily Bread and Pita. It was just two blocks away.

I was about as happy as a cat in a car wash. Here's the thing. No one had to babysit for my brother Billy. He worked at a gas station after school. Daniel and Nick were staying at Barney Fodstock's all week. Hillary got to stay home because she was a "responsible teenager."

As if!

Me? I was the youngest. "The baby." So I had to be baby-sat. I mean, I liked Mike and Mary's. But I was tired of being bossed around.

Mike waved from inside the store. "How ya doing, sport?" he greeted me. He held up an open palm. "Slap me high!"

I jumped up and gave him a high five.

He lowered his hand to waist level. "Slap me low."

I moved to give him a low five, but he pulled his hand away. "Too sloooow!" Mike gushed, laughing.

"Again," I demanded.

This time, I was ready for him. *Slap!*

"Yow! That stung," Mike exclaimed, shaking his hand. "You're getting pretty tough in your old age."

I smiled. It was hard to stay miserable with Mike around. But I'd try.

Mary gave me a hug. "It's good to see you, Jigsaw. It'll be fun to have you around this week."

A detective is like a scientist. He must train himself to be *observant.* I noted the little things, the small details. I looked around the shop with the careful eye of a detective.

There was a long glass counter on the left. Behind that, there was food, the cash register, the yogurt machine, and a big refrigerator filled with cold drinks. On the right, there were a few tables with plastic chairs. That was about it.

Some customers straggled in. "You keep Jigsaw company," Mike told Mary. "I'll take care of this." Mike hustled behind the counter and took their orders. He chatted with the customers and made them laugh. Everybody liked Mike. He claimed it was because he's short and bald. Go figure.

Mary sat down with me. She had long blond hair and eyes as green as AstroTurf. "What's the matter?" she asked. "You seem quiet."

"I like coming here," I answered. "But . . . well . . . I'm tired of being treated like a baby. Everybody else in my family gets to do what they want."

Mary chewed on her lower lip. "Don't let it bother you, Jigsaw. We'll have fun. You'll see."

I slipped the poster out of my backpack. "Can I tape this to your wall? It's for our detective business."

"Sure," Mary answered, eyeing the poster. "You know, maybe it's a good thing you're here. We've had problems lately. I've been thinking about calling the police."

Chapter Four

The Missing Brownies

"The police?!" I exclaimed.

A few customers turned their heads. I recognized some of them from school. There was Bigs Maloney and Lucy Hiller, Shirley Hitchcock, Bobby-Sue Black, and Jake "The Snake" O'Brien. It seemed like everybody came to Mike and Mary's for after-school snacks. Mary's double-chunk chocolate chip cookies were famous.

"Shhh," Mary whispered. "We'll talk later. I've got work to do."

I killed time by walking around the block.

I saw a few kids hanging around by the Dumpster. They were teenagers. It looked like hanging around and doing nothing was their specialty. I made a note of it in my detective journal. I already knew how to spell teenager:

T-R-O-U-B-L-E.

When I returned to the store, all the customers had gone. The after-school rush was over. Mary gestured toward the poster on the wall. She told Mike, "I'm going to hire Jigsaw."

Mike grumbled. But before he could complain, Mary slapped a five-dollar bill on the table.

"Abraham Lincoln," I murmured. "My favorite president."

"It's all yours . . ." Mary said, "if you can catch the brownie bandit."

I wrote in my detective journal:

CLIENTS: MIKE AND MARY.

Below that I wrote,

STOLEN BROWNIES.

"Give me the facts," I told Mary.

She pointed to a large plate on the counter. It was filled with desserts. "It's been going on for about a week now. Every afternoon, we're a few brownies short."

"Are you sure?" I asked.

Mary nodded. "Definitely. This place gets crowded when school lets out. When it slows down, I always notice that there's a couple of brownies missing."

Mary continued, "Lately, we've even run out of brownies. It's bad business. I'm afraid we might lose customers to the store down the block, Barney Black's Sweet Shop. If kids can't get their brownies here, they might shop somewhere else."

I nodded. Mike seemed worried. If kids started going to Barney's, then Mike and Mary would be out of business.

All this talk was making me hungry. "I think I'll need to take a closer look at one of those brownies. It may be a clue."

I bit into a brownie. "We're dealing with a smart thief," I concluded. "These brownies are terrific. Moist, yet chewy."

I soon realized that I'd gobbled up the

whole brownie. "I'll need more evidence," I told Mary. "Can I have another brownie? And may I please have some grape juice, too?"

"Do you think the juice is a clue?" Mike asked.

"Nope. Just thirsty."

Mary laughed. She gave me another brownie and a large grape juice.

"Aren't you guys eating?" I asked.

Mike glanced sadly at Mary. She shook her head. "We're both on strict diets. No more sweets for us."

Mike rubbed his round belly. "We're trying to lose weight."

"Do you have any suspects?" I asked.

"Not really," Mike replied. "We get a lot of people in here. The thief could be anybody."

Mike glanced at his watch. He walked to the door and flipped down a sign: CLOSED.

"We'd better clean up and get you home," he declared.

I thought about the case while helping Mike mop the floor. This was going to be a tough one. A lot of the kids who came here knew me. Plus, my poster — with my picture — was hanging on the wall. No thief was going to try any funny stuff with a top detective hanging around. I decided to go

undercover. And I didn't mean climbing into bed.

I stopped to scribble in my journal:

THE CASE OF THE DETECTIVE IN DISGUISE.

But what disguise should I wear?

Chapter Five

Zigzag Message

Ms. Gleason kept us hopping on Tuesday. No, she didn't give us pogo sticks. But I learned so much that my head grew two hat sizes. First, we did an experiment for our weather unit. We used the scientific method. We had to make *observations* — just like a detective. I knew more about rain, sleet, and snow than our mail carrier, Doris.

Today we studied thunder and lightning.

At circle time, Ms. Gleason read to us about Martin Luther King, Jr. He was a true American hero. He believed in equality for everybody, no matter what. Ms. Gleason said that the whole school would be decorating the halls this week.

"Why?" asked Ralphie Jordan.

"Think about it, Ralphie," Ms. Gleason said. "What might we be hanging in the halls this week?"

Ralphie's face broke into a loopy smile. "Our underwear?!"

"Oh, Ralphie," groaned Ms. Gleason.

Everybody laughed at Ralphie's joke. After all, *underwear* was just one of those funny words. All the kids in class laughed whenever we heard it. *Stinky* — that was another funny word. Put them together, *stinky underwear,* and suddenly you've got a classroom full of kids rolling on the floor, laughing their heads off.

Ms. Gleason asked us, "Whose birthday are we celebrating next week?"

"I know!" Danika Starling exclaimed. "Martin Luther King, Jr.'s!"

"That's right, Danika," Ms. Gleason said. "Our principal, Mr. Rogers, gave room 201 a special assignment. We'll be decorating the banner for the lobby."

Ms. Gleason pulled out a long roll of paper. It read:

JOIN HANDS FOR KINDNESS AND JUSTICE!

I raised my hand. "Can I color it?"

"Me, too!" Bigs Maloney said.

"No, me!" Lucy Hiller shouted.

"Slow down, everybody," Ms. Gleason said, laughing. "All of you will get a chance to color in a letter. Ralphie, Kim, Mike, Athena — bring the banner and crayons into the hall. When you finish a letter, pick someone to replace you. Everybody else, take out your writing folders."

Before I started on my story, I jotted a quick note to Mila. It was in code:

C N O S L E Y Y T R C D
A Y U O V M M S E Y O E

It was called a zigzag code. The words were written up and down on two lines. I wrote the first letter, C. Beneath it, I wrote the second letter, A. Then I started on the first line again. To make it a little tougher, I didn't put any spaces between the words.

I handed the note to Mila. A moment later, she smiled and slid a finger across her nose. That was our secret signal. She understood the message.

Soon our fifth-grade buddies were coming through the door. Ms. Gleason sent half of our class down the hall to meet with their buddies in Mr. Alonzo's fifth-grade classroom. That's how everybody fit.

I watched as the fifth-graders came in. There was Jimmy the Weasel, Rajib Manna, Henry Sosa, and Scooby Wendell. There was Bobbie-Sue Black, Babs Barbo, Silu Chang, and Kelsey Saperstein, giggling as usual. And, of course, my buddy Ben Ewing.

The minute I saw Ben, I knew something was wrong.

Chapter Six

A Stone in My Shoe

We got started on our projects right away. First, we traced our hand on a piece of construction paper. Then our fifth-grade buddies cut it out very carefully. Fifth-graders are good at that stuff.

Ms. Gleason explained, “Our entire school is celebrating Martin Luther King, Jr.’s birthday. We’re calling it the Peace and Kindness Challenge. We’re asking every student to think about what you could do to make a more peaceful world.”

"Could it be *anything* we want?" Geetha asked.

"Yes," Ms. Gleason answered. "Like Martin Luther King, I want you all to dream of a better world. Think about what YOU can do to help. Talk it over with your buddies. Then write your answer on the helping hands. Every class in school is doing it. We'll hang our hands up and down the halls."

After a lot of discussion, we had a great collection of ideas. Everyone except me. I wasn't so sure that I could make a better world all by myself. After all, I was a detective, not Hercules. Here's what everybody else wrote:

I will make the world a better place by helping the homeless.

— Lucy

I will be a doctor and help sick people.

— Geetha

I will talk to kids who don't have anyone to talk to.

— Jasper

Plant flowers everywhere!

— Joey

If someone punches me I won't punch back.

— Helen

I will stand Up for people.

— Bigs

I could create world peace by

making friends.

— Danika

By putting a smile on my face!

— Athena

We should protect animals around the world.

— Nicole

I will not push in the cubbies.

— Bobby

Talk to kids who are lonely.

— Ralphie

I am going to pick up litter.

— Kim

I WILL BE NICE ON THE PLAYGROUND.
— MIKE

I don't think people should be made fun of.
— Eddie

I will give food to poor people.
— Mila

Unfortunately, my buddy Ben wasn't much help. He was too miserable. I tried to cheer him up. I made goofy faces. I cracked jokes. I even fell off my chair on purpose. But nothing worked.

"What's wrong?" I finally asked.

"Someone stole my football," Ben said.

"Mila and I will help you get it back," I offered.

Suddenly Bobby Solofsky nudged me out of the way. "I'm a better detective

than him," Bobby bragged. "I'll find your football."

Oh, brother. Mr. Wonderful — Bobby Solofsky. He'd been a stone in my shoe since kindergarten. Solofsky always tried to trick me. And he always failed. I wondered what he was up to this time.

"Forget it, guys," Ben said, shaking his head sadly. "My ball is gone forever."

"Don't give up," I urged. "I'll help you get justice!"

"Don't listen to him." Bobby snorted. "I *guarantee* I'll find that football for you."

"Who invited you, Solofsky?" I snarled.

"Guys! Guys!" Ben interrupted. "I don't care who solves the case. Just get my football back. Please."

"May the best detective win," Bobby said. He smiled wickedly. "And that means me!"

Chapter Seven

Red Cap

Instead of going straight into Our Daily Bread that afternoon, I decided to swing around the back and have another look around. There was a small parking lot behind the store, with enough room for about twenty cars. There was a big brown Dumpster. Beyond the lot were the backyards of a few houses. As I guessed, I saw the same kids as yesterday. It didn't look like a meeting of Boy Scout Troop #67, if you know what I mean. Yeesh, teenagers.

I gave Mike and Mary's back door a pull.

Nothing doing. I yanked harder. The heavy, metal door didn't budge. Good, I thought to myself. The thief isn't sneaking in the back door.

"They keep it locked," a voice said.

I glanced over my shoulder. A boy with a red cap stood nearby. "What are you doing, short stuff?" he asked.

I looked him up and down. There was a lot of "up" to look at. This kid was tall, all right. I decided to get out of there, fast. The next thing I remember, Red Cap grabbed me by the shoulder. "Hey, I asked a question," he snarled. "Why are you poking around back here?"

Red Cap gave my shoulder a *squeeze*. I felt like an orange. "If you're trying to get juice out of me," I said, "it's not going to work."

The boy's dark eyes pierced through me. He grinned, then let go of my shoulder.

"Get lost," he said. "Scram."

So, well, I scrammed. It wasn't like I enjoyed his company.

When I got back, the store was jammed with customers. I strolled in, nodded at Mike, and kept right on walking. I didn't want anyone to notice me. I stepped into the back room.

When I came back out five minutes later, even my pet parakeet wouldn't have recognized me. Of course, I didn't have a pet parakeet. But never mind that. I wore a long, tan raincoat. I turned up the collar, pulled a hat over my eyes, and shoved my hands deep into the pockets.

A fake beard covered my face.

Sure, I may have looked strange. But no one could tell that I was a detective in disguise. I sat with my back to the counter and slipped on the rearview sunglasses. They were like regular glasses, except small mirrors were taped to the lenses. This way, I could face forward but still see what was going on behind me! I opened a comic book and pretended to read. I had a perfect view of the dessert tray.

For the next hour, I tried to observe everything. A steady stream of customers flowed into the store. I never took my eyes off the brownies. It was the perfect setup. Except for one thing. The fake beard made me hotter than a woolly mammoth in a pizza oven.

Mike had been right. The store did get all

SUPER SPY

kinds of people. But the only ones touching the brownies were Mike and Mary.

I made notes in my journal. I saw that Bobby-Sue Black was here again. She bought a brownie.

It made me wonder.

Suddenly, I stiffened. A familiar voice said: "I saw a kid snooping around out back," the voice told Mike. "I figured you should know about it."

It was Red Cap.

Chapter Eight

Undercover

That night I talked to Mila on the phone. I told her about Ben's stolen football. "The problem is, I'm stuck at the sandwich shop all week. You've got to look for clues without me.

"Try to find witnesses," I advised. "Bobby lives across the street from Ben. Mike Radcliffe lives near Ben, too. Talk to Mike. Poke around. Something will turn up."

"You can count on me," Mila replied. Then she asked, "How's your case coming?"

"Don't ask," I said.

"I just did," she stated.

Oh, brother. "I wouldn't call it a good day," I said. "Two more brownies were stolen — but I didn't see it happen. The store gets so crowded, it's hard to see everything. Some teenager with a red cap nearly squeezed me to a pulp. And I've got a rash on my face from wearing that lousy beard."

"I'd call that a bad day," Mila said.

"Let me ask you something," I said. "Bobby-Sue Black — what do you know about her?"

"Very little," Mila said. "She's in Mr. Alonzo's class. Why?"

"Do you know Barney Black's Sweet Shop?" I asked.

"Sure," Mila said. "It has great candy. But you should ask Bobby-Sue about that. Barney Black is her father."

"Her father!" I exclaimed. "Then why was she buying a brownie at Mike and Mary's?"

"Don't ask me," Mila said. "Ask Bobby-Sue."

I made a few more notes in my journal. I wrote the name Bobby-Sue Black and circled it. Could she be the one stealing the brownies? I couldn't be sure. But I knew Mila was right. I'd have to have a little talk with Bobby-Sue.

I came up with a better disguise the next day. I put on an apron and carried around a broom. It looked like I had a job cleaning

up. But I was really a bodyguard for a plate of brownies.

I had to admit it. I was beginning to like hanging around the store. It didn't feel like being baby-sat at all. Mike and Mary were fun. They had goofy nicknames for all the customers.

For example, there was Warm Cookie Guy. He came in at 3:30 every day and ordered the exact same thing. He liked his cookie warmed up in the microwave. It drove Mary nuts. Mike's favorite was the Sourpuss. She was a thin, sad-eyed lady who was always angry about something — the weather (too cold), the work (too busy), even the brownies (too fattening).

"What about the tall kid with the red cap?" I asked.

Mike smiled. "Oh, that's Marc. Real good kid. He lives in one of the houses behind the parking lot."

"I better have a talk with him," I remarked. "I don't trust teenagers."

Mike laughed. "That's funny, because Marc doesn't trust you, either. He came in here yesterday and told me he saw a suspicious kid out back. Just being a good neighbor, I guess."

"I guess," I answered.

I began to get into the routine of the store. Certain things happened every day. Mike *always* threw out the empty boxes in the afternoon. Then we always sat down together for a snack before cleanup. Mike called it our time "to shoot the breeze." Mike was a great talker. He could carry on a two-way conversation all by himself. It was a good thing. Because half the time Mary wasn't even listening.

Mike took a small bite of his granola bar, then tossed it into the garbage can. "Tastes like tree bark," he complained. "I'm starving, Mary! I hate this diet! I don't want

GRANOLA

to be skinny and miserable. I'd rather be plump and jolly."

Just then, Bobby Solofsky came into the store with Mike Radcliff. "Hey, Theodore," he crowed. "Any luck finding Ben's football?"

I didn't bother to reply.

Solofsky laughed, like he already knew the answer. "I didn't think so, *Theodore*!" I hated when he called me that. They bought vanilla milk shakes, then left the store.

It was how I liked Solofsky best: *Leaving*.

Chapter Nine

Counting Alligators

I forgot my lunch on Thursday. That meant I had to eat the hot lunch — a cheeseburger that looked like it was left over from the Jurassic period.

"I'd rather eat an old shoe," I groaned.

Helen Zuckerman plopped down beside me. It could only mean one thing. Helen had a new joke to tell. "Hey, Jigsaw," Helen said. "How do they stop crime at McDonald's?"

I shrugged.

"With a burger alarm!" Helen shouted. "Get it? *Burger alarm!*"

I got it and told her so.

Mila sat down opposite us. I was relieved. “How’s our case coming?” I asked her.

Mila told me all about it. Ben Ewing said he left his football outside by accident. In the morning, the football was gone.

“Any clues?”

“Not much,” Mila said. I could hear the frustration in her voice. “There’s one thing bothering me, though. Every time I see

Mike Radcliff, he's too busy too talk. I'm beginning to think he's avoiding me."

I told Mila about the brownie bandit. "I don't know who's doing it," I admitted. "The only people I've seen touching the brownies are Mike and Mary."

"Hmmm," Mila said.

I wanted to ask her what "hmmm" meant. Was it a good "hmmm" or a bad "hmmm"? But I wanted to escape from Helen's jokes even more. One bad joke a day was enough for me.

I caught up with Bobby-Sue Black by the bike racks after school. I told her that I'd seen her in Mike and Mary's store.

"And? So?" Bobby-Sue said with a yawn.

"So I'm wondering why you bought a brownie at Mike and Mary's. That is, IF you bought it."

Bobby-Sue scowled. "Whaddya mean . . . *if* I bought it?"

Bobby-Sue knew exactly what I meant. "I

don't steal, if that's what you are trying to say," she said firmly.

Finally, she sighed. "Look, if you tell my father, I'm dead. But Mary's brownies are delicious. I'd rather pay for hers than eat my dad's for free."

"Moist and chewy," I said.

"Yup," Bobby-Sue agreed. "My dad's brownies are as dry as sawdust." She paused. “You won’t tell anyone I said that, will you?”

“My lips are sealed,” I answered. And that was that. She might be the thief, she might not. But by the look in her eyes, I’d say she was an honest person.

That afternoon I disguised myself as a football player. I watched Mike and Mary’s customers come and go. There were twenty brownies sold. But by the end of the day, there was an extra one missing. Something was wrong. A piece of the puzzle was missing. Then it hit me. I remembered my words to Mila: “The only people touching the brownies are Mike and Mary.”

It was true. Except for today. Mary’s customers didn’t buy any brownies. She never touched them. Just then, Mike left to throw out the garbage. I watched the clock carefully. He returned after four minutes and twenty-six seconds. I jotted it down in my journal:

4 minutes, 26 seconds
Check it out

I decided to retrace his steps. I walked down the basement steps. Out the back door. Over to the Dumpster. Then back again. I counted to myself the whole time: "One alligator, two alligator, three alligator . . ."

I was back inside after seventy-four alligators. I did the math in my journal. One minute was sixty alligators.

74 - 60 = 14

It took me only one minute and fourteen seconds. Why did the same trip take Mike almost four and a half minutes?

It was time to make peace with Red Cap,

er, I mean, Marc. I didn't see him at first, until I looked up. He was leaning out of his second-floor window, just watching the world go by. It gave me an idea.

I called him down and we had a little chat. It turned out that Mike was right. Marc was a good guy, once you got to know him. I told him I was a detective working on a case. We talked about the stolen brownies. I offered him a dollar if he'd help me.

Marc said he'd do it for free.

"See you tomorrow," I said.

Marc winked. "Sure thing . . . Detective Jones."

Chapter Ten

Strange Weather

The next morning, Mila and I saw Bobby Solofsky on the bus. He sat in the back with Mike Radcliff. They seemed as happy as dentists at a candy store.

When the bus dropped us off, Bobby and Mike raced in our direction. "Hey, guys. Wait up."

"What now, Solofsky?" I groaned.

Bobby waved at Ben Ewing across the school yard. "Show him!" Bobby shouted.

Ben smiled brightly. He reached into his

backpack and pulled out his prized football. "Catch!" he said to me.

I dropped the ball.

"Poor Theodore," Bobby said. "It looks like you fumbled the case this time."

Bobby pulled out a crisp, clean, five-dollar bill. "Ben gave it to me," Bobby said. "Because I'm such a great detective."

Then he laughed.

Long and loud.

It was like talking to Helen Zuckerman.

I didn't see what was so funny.

"Not so fast, Solofsky," Mila said. "Something fishy is going on around here. How did you solve the case?"

"Easy," Bobby bragged. "Mike was a witness. He saw the kids do it."

Mike chimed in. "I saw the whole thing from my bedroom window."

Mila was right. This case was fishy. In fact, it smelled like Sea World. Sure, Mike Radcliff was a decent guy. But he'd do anything Bobby told him. I didn't trust him.

Mike explained that he saw three big kids walk on Ben's lawn. They took the ball, then hid it in the bushes. Mike said he went out and got the ball before the kids had time to come back for it.

"Maybe that's what happened," I said. "But why did you wait so long before giving the ball back?"

Bobby put his arm around Mike's

shoulders. “Mike was scared,” Bobby said. “Those teenagers were awful big.”

I didn’t argue. “What time was it when you saw them?”

Mike glanced at Bobby. “About, um, eight-thirty.”

“You must be part owl,” I said. “Because it’s hard to see in the dark.”

“It was a full moon,” Bobby quickly replied.

"Not quite, Solofsky," Mila replied. "The clouds were too thick on Monday night. You remember all that rain we had. Besides, I checked the neighborhood. The nearest streetlight was broken."

Even Ben seemed a little curious now. "Why did they *hide* the football, anyway? Why didn't they just take it? I don't get it."

Bobby waved a hand, like swatting away a pesky fly. "When the thieves picked up the football, a set of car headlights turned up the street. They must have decided to ditch the stolen ball until later."

"Your story is like Swiss cheese," I said. "It's full of holes. What I want to know is: *How did Mike see in the dark?*"

All eyes turned to Mike Radcliff. He swallowed hard and stammered, "I was, um, reading at my desk. And, um, I guess I fell asleep. Then suddenly, I awoke to a

crash of thunder. And I looked out the window. Lightning lit the sky. That's when I saw the teenagers take the ball."

"That's pretty strange weather," I said. "The thunder woke you up. Then the lightning came. And then you saw the robbers?"

"What's the matter, Theodore?" Bobby sniped. "Do you need me to explain it in slow motion? Yes, he heard thunder. Yes, he looked out the window. Yes, there was lightning. Yes, he saw the robbers. Case closed. Mystery solved."

Mila angrily jabbed a finger at Solofsky. "You guys are lying — and I can prove it!"

Chapter Eleven

With a Little Help from My Friends

Bobby shook his head. "Let's go, Mike. We're not sticking around for this."

"Oh, yes you are," Ben threatened.

Bobby and Mike didn't dare move.

"Go on, Mila," Ben said politely.

Mila folded her arms across her chest. "We've been studying weather in Ms. Gleason's class," she told Ben.

"We learned about light and sound. Light travels faster than sound. Mike's story doesn't hold up. He said he awoke to thunder. Then he saw lightning. Weather

doesn't work that way. Lightning always comes first. That's why I know he's lying."

Solofsky stood tight-lipped. He wasn't going to say a word. But Mike Radcliff looked at Ben towering over him and turned pale. "It was all Bobby's idea!" Mike confessed. "He wanted to fake a crime. Then he'd solve it and be the hero!"

In a gush of words, Mike explained everything. He saw the football on the lawn with Bobby. They decided to "borrow" it. "Bobby was jealous," Mike explained to Ben. "He didn't like that you were becoming friends with Jigsaw."

Ben shook his head sadly. Then he held out his hand. "Cough it up, Bobby," he demanded.

Solofsky pulled out a five-dollar bill. Ben plucked it from his fingertips and handed it to Mila. "Thanks," Ben told her. "You deserve it."

One mystery solved.

One more to go.

I ran to the store right after school. I met Marc in the parking lot and lent him a walkie-talkie. The plan was set. Marc went up to his back window and waited for my signal.

As usual, Mike went outside to throw out the garbage at around five o'clock. The moment he left, I reached for my walkie-talkie.

“He’s on his way,” I whispered.

“I hear you loud and clear,” Marc replied. “Over and out.”

Mike returned about five minutes later.

A few minutes after that, Marc strolled in the front door. He looked at me and winked.

I nodded back.

Marc and I walked up to Mike and Mary. “We just solved the case,” I announced.

Mary’s eyebrow lifted.

Mike’s jaw dropped.

“It took me a while,” I admitted, looking directly at Mike. “It never occurred to me that you’d be stealing from yourself.”

It’s always the little things that give a thief away. I picked a brownie crumb off Mike’s collar. “Some diet,” I said. “Every day you sneak a brownie or two into an empty box. When you go outside to throw out the garbage, you have a little snack.”

"But . . ." Mike stammered.

"Marc saw everything," I said. "Don't bother denying it."

Mary didn't seem too mad. To tell the truth, she didn't even seem all that surprised. She just shook her head and laughed.

Mike tried to defend himself. "Mary, darling, poopsie doll. You can't blame me. Everybody knows that you make the best brownies in the world. I couldn't help myself!"

Mary slipped a brownie off the plate and popped a piece into her mouth. "Oh, well," she said, giving Mike a big hug. "I guess I like my men plump and jolly. No more diets for you!"

My mom came and picked me up a little later. She loved hearing about the brownie bandit. I hadn't seen her laugh so hard in a long while. "We'd better get going," she said. "It's starting to snow."

"Snow?!"

I raced to the window. A few white flakes fluttered from the clouds. The case was over. In one day, we'd solved two mysteries. And I'd made a new friend — a teenager, no less. And like Martin Luther King, Jr., I suddenly knew how to make the world a better place.

The same way I do puzzles.

The same way I solve mysteries.

Just one piece at a time.

The Case of the Bicycle Bandit

For Danny Evans and Sam Lewis

Chapter One

Old Rusty

"Wait up, Jigsaw!" Ralphie Jordan cried out. "My bike chain slipped off!"

Oh, brother. Not again.

The town library was five minutes from my house. Four minutes if the wind was right. But today it was taking forever — all because of Ralphie Jordan's bicycle.

Ralphie called it "Old Rusty."

I would have called it "Old Hunk of Junk."

Old Rusty could shake and rattle. But it couldn't roll. Not very well, anyway. Its tires were bent. Spokes were missing. The handlebars were twisted. The seat was ripped. The fenders rattled. The brakes squeaked. And worst of all, the chain kept falling off the whatchamacallit. After every block, Ralphie had to stop. He got off, turned the bicycle upside down, and carefully slipped the chain back onto the round thingy.

I turned and rode back to Ralphie. He was a mess. Grease from the chain covered his face, shirt, and hands. "Maybe we should go home," I offered.

"Hang on," Ralphie said. "Old Rusty will get me there." Ralphie patted Old Rusty on the, er, *rust*, and away we zoomed. At least, I zoomed. Old Rusty sort of crawled. Banging and clanging all the way.

Our teacher, Ms. Gleason, had given us book reports for homework. We had to find a book in the library, read it, and write about it. The book had to be *at least* eighty pages long.

COBRA
DAREDEVIL

Ralphie chained our bikes to the bike rack and we headed inside. I wandered into the mystery section. Ralphie seemed to wander all over. First, Ralphie stared into the fish tank, making goofy faces and *glub-glub* sounds. Then he walked along, picked up a book, turned to the last page, frowned, and put it back. Over and over again.

"What are you doing, Ralphie?" I asked.

"Just looking," he said.

"What kind of book are you looking for?"

"A short one," Ralphie replied. "And I just found it." He held up a book. It was called *Plastic: Yesterday, Today, and Tomorrow.*

"You want to do a report on . . . plastic?" I asked.

Ralphie opened the book to the last page. "Look, exactly eighty pages — and it has lots of pictures, too."

I sighed and kept searching in the

mystery section. After all, I was a detective. For a dollar a day, I made problems go away. I loved everything about mysteries — the clues, the secret codes, the disguises, everything. I even loved mystery stories. I picked out an Encyclopedia Brown.

We checked out our books and went outside.

At the bike rack, Ralphie stopped suddenly. “My bike!” he exclaimed. “It’s g-g-gone!”

Chapter Two

The Scene of the Crime

Ralphie's lower lip trembled. He blinked back tears. "Where's Old Rusty?" he asked me.

But Ralphie already knew the answer. He just couldn't believe it. Somebody had stolen Ralphie's bike.

I was lucky. My bike was still there.

I pulled my detective journal from my backpack. I wrote:

THE CASE OF THE BICYCLE BANDIT

"Wait here," I told Ralphie. I pulled a quarter out of my pocket. "Don't touch anything. I'm going inside to call Mila. We'll need her help."

I told Mila to get down to the library, fast.

"How fast?" she asked.

"Like, yesterday," I replied.

"I'll be right there," Mila answered.

I went back outside. Ralphie was sitting on the ground, cross-legged. His chin was buried in his hands.

While we waited for Mila, I drew a quick sketch. When you're a detective, it's

important to study the scene of the crime. That's how you find clues. There were five bicycles in the rack. Mine was brand-new, not a hand-me-down like Ralphie's. I used to ride my brother Nicholas's beat-up old bike. Then I helped pay for a new one with the money I earned from my detective business. It was a Cobra Daredevil with a banana-yellow frame.

"That's weird," I said. "Isn't this your lock, Ralphie?"

Ralphie nodded. "Yeah."

"I thought you locked up *both* bikes."

"I did," Ralphie answered.

I didn't argue. But facts were facts. Here was my bike, locked up with Ralphie's chain. His bike was gone. Maybe Ralphie had locked up only my bike by mistake.

Mila pulled up, slamming on the brakes. Her back wheel skidded on the cement. Ralphie barely noticed. He stared at the empty space in the bike rack, frowning.

COBRA
DAREDEVIL

Mila is my partner. Together, we solve mysteries. We've found missing hamsters, stolen baseball cards, lost sleds. We've even tangled with phoney lake monsters and runaway dogs. But a stolen bicycle — that was something new. "All right," she said. "Tell me what happened."

I told Mila what we knew. She listened carefully, arms folded across her chest. "The bandit was lucky," I said. "It looks like Ralphie forgot to lock his bicycle."

Mila nodded. "*Looks* that way."

Ralphie protested. "Don't blame me. I locked up *both* bikes. I know I did. *I know it.*"

Mila bit her lip. She put her hand on Ralphie's shoulder. "No one is blaming you," she soothed. "You're right to feel mad. Stealing a bicycle — that's like the worst thing on earth. Only a real creep would do something like that."

Ralphie sniffed and looked away. His eyes followed a bird circling in the sky. It

circled once, twice, three times. Then it flew off.

Leaving behind an empty sky.

"A real creep," Ralphie muttered in agreement.

Chapter Three

Witnesses

"What time is it?" I asked.

Ralphie glanced at his bare wrist. "Half past my freckle," he gloomily replied.

I couldn't help but smile. And Ralphie couldn't help but say funny things. With him, it was like breathing. Ralphie even made jokes when nobody felt like laughing.

"Let's see if there were any witnesses," Mila suggested. She gestured toward the grassy lawn beyond the bike racks. There was a lady walking a small dog with shaggy white fur. That is, the *dog* had shaggy white

fur. The lady's hair was shaggy and black. There was a freckle-faced teenager with red hair leaning against a tree. I caught him looking in our direction. He quickly turned away to watch some girls playing Frisbee. Behind us, a man on a bench sat reading a newspaper. A round hat sat beside him, like an old friend.

I turned to Ralphie. "You better leave the detective work to us," I said. "Do you want to borrow my bike to get home?"

Ralphie shook his head. "No, I'll walk. Might as well get used to it." Ralphie's eyes suddenly widened. "Hey, there's David Chang. He's on my brother Justin's basketball team. Maybe I can walk home with him."

Ralphie ran up to David, who was leaving the library. I watched Ralphie gesture and point to the bike rack. He was telling David the whole sad story. I walked over. Ralphie introduced us. "Jigsaw is a detective," Ralphie bragged. "He'll get my bike back."

David looked about fourteen years old. He had a helmet in one hand and a skateboard under the other arm. David shifted uncomfortably under the weight of his backpack. I asked him if he had noticed anyone strange inside the library. "Nah, I just dropped off a few books and scrammed," he answered. "It's too nice to hang inside."

I watched them walk away. Actually, only Ralphie walked. David cruised alongside

him on his skateboard. He stopped, handed Ralphie his backpack, and got back on the skateboard. What a guy, I thought. David made Ralphie carry his heavy backpack!

Across the field, Mila was standing with the lady and her dog. Mila bent down and tried to pet the dog. But it was one of those tiny, nervous dogs. It yapped at Mila and snapped its sharp little teeth. Mila pulled her hand away and growled back.

The man on the bench was nice enough. He said he'd been reading and hadn't seen anything. He laughed. "Once I start reading, we could have an earthquake and I wouldn't notice."

I thanked him anyway. I wrote his name in my journal, just in case: **MAX KORNSTEIN**. When I turned around, Mila was talking to the Frisbee players. They seemed to be shaking their heads. The red-haired boy stood up to leave on his skateboard. "Wait up!" I called. "I need to talk to you!"

The boy glanced over his shoulder. He put a hand to his ear and shook his head. Like he couldn't hear me. Then he pushed off hard with his right foot. *Zoom.*

He left me in the dust.

Go figure.

Chapter Four

Suspect on Wheels

I awoke Sunday morning to find a note on my doorstep.

tree	house	the	case	message
the	at	of	destroy	secret
in	noon	facts	this	the
meet	to	the	note	solve
let's	go	over	after	you

I started reading it: *tree house the case message the at of . . .*

It didn't make any sense. That could only

mean one thing. It was a message from Mila. She always wrote her notes in code.

I searched my brain for all the codes I knew. Believe me, it was crowded in there. Secret codes are a part of the business. You can't be a detective without them. I knew mirror codes and color codes, space codes and list codes. Suddenly it hit me. This was an up-and-down code. Instead of reading from left to right, you had to start at the bottom of the first column, read up, then go over to the next column and read down, then over, then up again.

I figured out the message. Then it was time to destroy the note. That's where my trusty dog, Rags, came in. He'd eat anything. I spread peanut butter on it. Rags was happy to help.

There was a full glass of grape juice waiting for Mila later that morning when she climbed the tree house ladder. She was singing "Let's Go Fly a Kite" from *Mary*

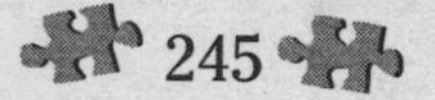

Poppins. As usual, she changed the words around:

"Let's go ride a bike
Up to the highest height!
Let's go ride a bike
And send it . . ."

Mila stopped singing and scratched her nose. "Hey, Jigsaw. What rhymes with *soaring*?"

"Pouring?" I offered. "Snoring?"

Mila sang again:

"Let's go ride a bike
It sure . . . beats . . . snoring!"

"You're nuts," I observed.

Mila shrugged. "Maybe."

"Let's get down to business," I said. "Any luck with the witnesses?"

"Not really," Mila said. "And I almost got bit, too," she added.

I smiled. "Yeah, that little dog seemed angry."

"Actually, the lady said the dog, Mr. Pickles, was scared."

"Scared of *you*?" I laughed.

"Not me," Mila said. "Mr. Pickles almost got run over by a skateboarder."

"Oh?"

"Yeah. The lady was upset about it. She said three kids came racing down the sidewalk and almost flattened Mr. Pickles."

"Three kids?" I asked. "On skateboards?"

Mila opened her little memo pad. She read out loud: "'Three teenagers on skateboards . . .'"

"I saw two kids with skateboards at the library," I recalled. "I wonder if it was them? And if it was, *who* was the third kid? And *where* was he?"

We let that question wander past like a lonely cloud. I suddenly remembered David Chang. His backpack was large and bulky. I told Mila about it.

"It must have been filled with books," Mila concluded.

"Nope," I said. "He told me he dropped off a few books and scrammed."

Mila twisted the ends of her long black hair. "Are you sure his backpack was full?"

"I think so," I said. "He made Ralphie carry it. We can check with him."

I wrote in my journal:

What was in David Chang's backpack?

Mila looked over my shoulder as I wrote. "David couldn't have stolen the bike. You saw him leave the library."

"Yes," I said. "But the lady saw *three* kids ride skateboards to the library. Only two

left on skateboards. What happened to the other kid?"

Mila stared at me, blinking. "Do you think . . . ?"

I nodded. It was exactly what I thought. "Maybe he's the one who took Ralphie's bicycle."

"But what about his skateboard?" Mila asked. "You can't ride a bike and carry a skateboard at the same time."

I gulped down the last of my grape juice. "I think David Chang may know the answer."

Chapter Five

Justin

We found Ralphie Jordan in his driveway. He was shooting hoops with his older brother, Justin.

Just as Ralphie went to shoot, Justin soared high into the air. *WHAP!* He blocked the shot and sent the ball flying into the bushes. Then Justin sank three long bombs — *swish, swish, swish* — and the game was over.

"I'm gonna beat you one day," Ralphie promised. "Just you wait."

Justin just laughed and gave Ralphie a

playful shove. Of course, we attacked. Ralphie pounced on Justin's legs. Mila jumped on his back, driving Justin to the ground. I twisted his fingers into pretzels.

"Need a hand?" a voice asked.

We stopped. It was David Chang.

"I've got it under control," Justin replied. *Wham, bam*. He stacked us up like pancakes and pinned us to the ground. It felt like he was a steamroller — and we were the road.

Ouch.

Justin stood up, puffing slightly. "You guys are getting tough," he said. "But not tough enough. I'd love to hang around, but I've got things to do."

He got his skateboard out of the garage. "Hey, Ralphie," he called out. "You can borrow my bike if you want."

"Maybe, sure, thanks," Ralphie mumbled.

"Hey, little brother," Justin said. "Don't stress about your bike. I'm sure it will turn up in a few days."

Ralphie frowned. "Old Rusty is gone forever," he sighed.

"No way," Justin said, jerking a thumb toward Mila and me. "You'll get Old Rusty back. You've got top detectives on the case." He gave us a wink.

"Where are you guys going, anyway?" Ralphie asked Justin and David.

"Out," Justin said. He strapped on his helmet.

I spoke up. "Do you guys know a kid with bright red hair? He's about your age, maybe older. He's got a lot of freckles."

David glanced at Justin.

"Lots of kids have freckles," Justin answered.

David wheeled around on his skateboard and raced down the driveway. Justin had fancier moves. He zigged and zagged,

leaning hard to his left then right. His arms were stretched out to his sides. Very cool.

"Your brother's nice," Mila observed.

"Yeah, most of the time," Ralphie agreed. "He likes to kid around a lot."

I laughed. "Remember the phony ghost? Justin had us fooled for a while."

We sat under a tree and laughed about it. A while back Justin pretended he was a

ghost. He had Ralphie nearly scared out of his boxer shorts. Fortunately, Mila and I solved the case.

Teenagers. Yeesh.

Ralphie wanted to pay us for our work. But there was one problem. He didn't get his allowance until the end of the week.

"This one's a freebie," I said. "But remember us if you win the lottery."

"Do you have any suspects?" Ralphie asked.

"Maybe," I answered. "There's one kid on a skateboard I'd like to track down. Unfortunately, the best witness is a dog named Mr. Pickles."

"Huh?"

"Don't worry about it, Ralphie," I said. "We'll get your bike back. I promise."

"One last thing, Ralphie," Mila said. "About David's backpack. Do you know what was in it?"

Ralphie tilted his head, thinking. "Oh, yeah. It was a skateboard."

"He had *two* skateboards?" I asked.

"Yeah," Ralphie said. "Weird, huh. He said he was holding it for a friend."

Mila and I exchanged looks.

"Weird, huh," she repeated.

I scratched the back of my neck. I had an itch to learn more about David Chang.

Chapter Six

Art Class

All the kids in room 201 were mad about Ralphie's bike.

"It's horrible!"

"It's terrible!"

"It's horribly terrible!"

"It's terribly horrible!"

They all promised to help. Everyone crowded around Ralphie, trying to cheer him up.

"Um, like, maybe your father will, like, buy you a new one," Lucy Hiller said.

"Don't want a new one," Ralphie flatly stated. "I like Old Rusty just fine. It was a hand-me-down from Justin. Besides, my dad says I can't get a new bike until my birthday."

"When's that?" Mila asked.

"July twelfth," groaned Ralphie. "About a million days from now."

"Have you tried begging?" Bobby Solofsky suggested.

Nicole Rodriguez piped up. "Bobby's right. Begging works. I learned that from our dog, Zippy. The trick is to try to look as much like a puppy as possible."

"Been there, done that," scoffed Ralphie. "I'm an expert." He dropped down to his knees, bent his hands before his chest like a hungry pooch, and whined, *"Nnnnn, nnnnn, nnnnn!"*

We all laughed. Ralphie brushed himself off. "Begging doesn't work with my dad. He just throws me a doggy snack."

LASTIC:
YESTERDAY
TODAY AND
TOMORROW

At recess, I fooled around on the monkey bars with Eddie Becker and Bigs Maloney.

"We don't get it," Eddie Becker said, hanging upside down by his knees. "Why would anybody steal Ralphie's bike?"

"It's a piece of junk," Bigs noted.

They were right. Why would anyone want a junker like Old Rusty? There's never a crime without a reason. What was the *motive*? Who would want an old, broken-down bicycle?

"Ralphie says he locked up *both* bikes," I said.

Bigs jumped to the ground. His big feet crashed like thunder. "No way," Bigs said. "The bandit would have taken your bike, Jigsaw. Your Cobra Daredevil is awesome."

I thanked Bigs for the kind words. The bell rang. We lined up to go inside. But a voice in my head kept repeating: *What if Ralphie was right about locking up both*

bikes? It was a piece I couldn't fit into the puzzle.

Ralphie had to be wrong, I concluded. No robber would unlock the bikes, take Ralphie's, then lock mine back up. It made no sense.

We had art with Mr. Manus on Mondays. Today, he encouraged us to draw whatever we wanted. I drew a picture of Rags.

Mr. Manus says we all have unique talents. Some people, like Joey Pignattano, are good at drawing flowers and trees. Kim Lewis is good at cars and trucks. And Geetha Nair, well, she can draw faces. That day, she drew an awesome picture of Bigs Maloney. It looked just like him.

Mr. Manus held it up for everyone to admire. “This goes up on the board,” he announced.

That's when Mila came up with a terrific idea. She whispered to Geetha, "Do you really want to help on the case?"

Geetha rarely spoke. She was very shy. Instead, she nodded.

Yes.

Chapter Seven

Geetha and Mr. Pickles

Yap, yap-yap! Bark-bark, barkbarkbarkbark!!!

I groaned into Mila's ear, "Mr. Pickles, I presume."

The door opened. The witness from the library, Mrs. Flint, smiled at Mila. Mr. Pickles jumped up and down by her feet, yapping loudly.

Bark-bark, grrrrr, barkbarkbarkbark!!!

Geetha stepped behind me.

"Don't worry about Mr. Pickles," Mrs. Flint said cheerfully. "He's just excited."

The little furball jumped up and down.

Mrs. Flint bent down until she was nose to nose with Mr. Pickles. "No, Mr. Pickles! NO!" she screamed.

"We don't mind," I lied. "Mr. Pickles is just, er, lively." I bent down to pet Mr. Pickles. He snapped at my hand like a hungry wolf.

"Down, Mr. Pickles! DOWN!" screamed Mrs. Flint. "I'm so sorry," she fretted, shoving Mr. Pickles away with her foot. "I'll put Mr. Pickles in the basement."

I thought that was a terrific idea.

Mrs. Flint led us to a screened back porch. It was filled with plants and strange flowers. "Welcome to my jungle," Mrs. Flint said, offering us lemonade and cookies.

"This is Geetha Nair," I explained, gesturing to Geetha. "She's an artist."

Geetha smiled politely at her shoes. She rested a large artist's pad on her lap. In her fist she clutched a bundle of colored pencils.

Mila explained the plan. We wanted Mrs.

Flint to describe the skateboarders. While she talked, Geetha would try to draw a picture of them.

"Oh, how thrilling!" Mrs. Flint said, snapping into a cookie. "Just like on television!"

I coughed. "This is for real," I reminded her.

We already knew the identity of the first skateboarder. That was David Chang. Mrs. Flint described him perfectly. I winked at Mila. Mrs. Flint was a good witness.

"What about the others?" I prodded.

Mrs. Flint gobbled down another cookie. A few crumbs fell to her lap. She closed her eyes and spoke: "Bright red hair . . . very curly . . . freckles . . . a little pug nose, like a piglet. . . ."

Geetha asked a few questions. She wanted to know the shape of his head, his eyes, his mouth. I looked at her sketchpad.

"Wow, that's him!" I said, remembering the boy at the library.

"Great," Mila said. "Now we can show the picture around. Somebody is bound to know his name."

"What about the third skateboarder?" I asked.

Mrs. Flint frowned. "He wore a sweatshirt with a hood. "I didn't get a good look at him."

The sweatshirt was dark green, she told us. And the boy was taller than the other two. That was all she knew. We gobbled down the last of the cookies and left.

Once outside, I turned to Mila. "We've got to find the third skateboarder."

Mila pointed at Geetha's picture of the red-haired boy. "Let's find *him* first. I think he'll lead us to the boy with the green sweatshirt."

"Great work," I thanked Geetha. "You've been a big help."

Geetha stared hard at the ground.

Slowly, ever so slightly, the corners of her mouth turned up into a smile.

Chapter Eight

The Hooded Rider

We made ten photocopies of Geetha's picture. Mila printed the words. Danika

Starling and Kim Lewis hung up the posters all over town. Everybody in our class chipped in for the reward — even Ms. Gleason.

I got a phone call the very next day.

It was from a third grader named Shirley Hitchcock. "I know the kid in the poster," she announced.

"Keep talking," I said.

"His name is Snarky Smithers. Everybody calls him the Snarkster."

"What's his address?" I asked.

"Do I get the reward?"

"Yes," I answered. "*After* you give me the address."

Shirley told me where he lived.

"How do you know him?" I asked.

"He lives on my block," Shirley explained.

"What else do you know?"

"He's a grease monkey," Shirley said.

"A grease monkey?"

"Yeah. The Snarkster loves building things. He takes things apart and puts them together again. Old radios, toasters, bicycles, go-carts . . ."

"Bicycles?" I asked. "What do you mean?"

Shirley told me that Snarky Smithers ran a little business. He bought old, junky bikes at garage sales — cheap. Then he fixed them up and sold them. "He's very talented," Shirley added.

I ate a bowl of Frosted Flakes in the kitchen. They tasted *grrreeat!* While I ate, I wrote in my detective journal. Like a jigsaw puzzle, the case was coming together. The clues were starting to fit into place.

THREE SUSPECTS
1) David Chang
2) Snarky Smithers
3) The Hooded Rider

I put a star next to number two. I asked myself, What do I know about Snarky Smithers?

I wrote down:

- Snarky builds bicycles.
- Motive? Spare parts!
- He could have used Old Rusty!

I began to wonder if it was a three-man job. I thought back to the day of the robbery. David Chang was *inside* the library. Snarky Smithers was *outside* the library. A witness saw David and Snarky together. But someone else took Old Rusty.

Maybe they all worked as a team.

Maybe David and Snarky were the lookouts.

It all depended on the hooded rider. We had to find him — soon.

I called Ralphie Jordan's house.

No one was home.

I had no luck at Mila's, either.

Oh, well. I'd have to go alone.

I went to the basement and spilled out my box of detective supplies. There it was — the Super Spy Scope X-2000. I pulled my cap down tight and left the house.

I was on my way to 211 Coconut Grove.

It was time to spy on Snarky Smithers.

Chapter Nine

The Stakeout

There was a tree across the street from 211 Coconut Grove. I pulled the straps on my backpack tight. Then up I climbed. A squirrel chittered angrily from a nearby branch. He didn't like sharing the tree, I supposed.

The X-2000 was the ultimate spying machine. It worked like binoculars. But it also had "special extender action." I could use it to see around corners.

In the detective business, we call this a stakeout. You watch and wait, hidden from

211

sight. Twenty minutes later the hooded rider rolled up on a skateboard. I couldn't see his face. He rang the doorbell. The door opened and there was the red-haired boy, Snarky Smithers. They walked together around the front of the house, opened the garage door, and went inside.

The door closed before I could get a good look inside. But I saw enough — bicycles, lots of bicycles. I saw that the garage had a side window. I counted to thirty. *One banana, two banana, three banana* . . . Then I jumped from the tree.

I made my way across the street. There were bushes on the side of the garage. I ducked down behind them. Ouch. Prickers. Slowly, silently, I pulled the X-2000 to its longest reach. I pointed the scope at the window.

The Snarkster faced the hooded rider. They were talking. Snarky was frowning, gesturing with his hands. The hooded

rider's back was to me. I wanted to put my ear to the windowpane to listen, but I didn't dare.

I felt something brush against me. I quickly spun around and lost my balance, tapping the X-2000 against the window. *Meow.* A black cat sat nearby, licking its paws. Bad, bad luck. I froze and held my breath.

Thirty bananas later, I peeked inside again. The Snarkster was gone! My eyes

searched from side to side. Did he hear me? Was he coming after me?

A door leading from inside the garage to the house opened. It was Snarky, coming back into the garage. He had something in his hand. The hooded rider held out a hand. One, two, three, four. Snarky counted out four dollar bills. They might have been ones, fives, or tens. I couldn't tell which. But one thing was sure: Snarky was paying him for something.

They shook hands and turned to leave. I made myself small behind the bushes. Crawling across the ground, I slid the scope of the X-2000 beyond the wall. The Snarkster yawned, scratched himself, and went into the house.

The hooded rider skateboarded down the driveway. Arms stretched out to his sides, he zigged and zagged, leaning hard to his left and right.

It hit me like a brick.

I knew the hooded rider.

Chapter Ten

Trapped!

I lay still for a few more minutes. Maybe I was waiting for the coast to clear. Maybe I was playing it safe. Or maybe I was just plain scared.

The garage was empty.

But the door was still open.

I knew what I had to do.

I took a deep breath and entered the garage.

It was cluttered with tools and bicycles. There was a pile of old tires. Spray-paint cans. Old bicycle parts strewn on the floor.

It was more like a workshop than a garage. There wasn't room for a car.

I crept up to the door that led into the house. I pressed my ear against it. I heard muffled sounds. The shuffling of feet. A chair scraping on the floor. The clink of a spoon against a dish. The kitchen, I decided. Snarky Smithers was in there, eating a snack.

I turned my gaze to the bicycles. I noticed one that looked familiar. Could it be? It *might* have been Old Rusty. But this bike wasn't rusty anymore. It had a new seat, new handlebars, new pedals. The spokes seemed shiny and clean. The frame was a shiny, sparkling blue. I sniffed it. Fresh paint. Still wet.

I was just about to get out of there when I heard a faint *clomp*, *clomp*. The sound of footsteps, coming closer, just on the other side of the door. I froze in place — and watched the doorknob slowly, slowly turn.

The Snarkster. He was coming into the garage!

I dove into the darkest corner and ducked down behind a few boxes. I heard the door open. Snarky entered the garage.

"Hmmmm, what's this?" he wondered aloud.

My heart beat faster. *Thumpa-thump, thumpa-thump, thumpa-thump.* I peeked around the box. Snarky was holding

something, turning it over in his hands. It was my Super Spy Scope X-2000! I'd left it on the ground beside Old Rusty. Snarky was suspicious. He looked around the garage. "Hello?" he called out. "Anybody here?"

He took a step toward me.

Then another.

Now my heart was a bass drum. *BOOM, BOOM, BOOM!* I closed my eyes and . . .

. . . *Bbbrrring. Bbbrrring-bbbring!*

The phone!

Answer it, I prayed. Go on, Snarky. Answer the phone!

Snarky paused. He looked toward the kitchen door. *Bbbrrring-bbbring*. He took another step toward me, muttered, then tossed the X-2000 onto a shelf. He went inside to answer the phone.

I didn't stick around to see what happened next. I jumped up — whoops, *CRASH!* — and knocked over a bicycle.

"Who's that?!" Snarky called out from the kitchen.

I grabbed the X-2000.

And never looked back.

I just ran. And ran. And ran.

Chapter Eleven

Confess!

My first stop was Mila's house.

We sat together on the steps of her front stoop. I told her about my adventures.

"Are you absolutely sure it was Justin?" Mila asked.

"Almost," I said. "All the clues point to him." I ticked them off on my fingers. "First, the way he rode the skateboard. It was just like Justin."

Mila went, "Hmmmm."

"Second, we already know that he's friends with David Chang. Third, I think

Ralphie was right all along. He *did* lock up both bikes. But it didn't matter."

"Explain," Mila said.

"Old Rusty was a hand-me-down," I said. "A hand-me-down bicycle with a hand-me-down lock. Justin knew the combination!"

"I get it," Mila said. "That's why your bike was still there. Justin locked it back up. He only wanted Old Rusty."

I flicked a pebble with my thumb. "Exactly."

"But . . . *why*?" Mila asked.

"Why?" I echoed.

"Why take his own brother's bike? Why not your bike? If he was going to sell it to this Snarkster fellow, wouldn't he get more money for a new bike?"

I frowned. "Please, Mila. Get real. I'm a detective. Nobody wants to steal from a detective.

"Anyway," I said glumly. "It has to be Justin. But we need more proof."

We found Ralphie and Justin at home, watching television. I asked to use the bathroom. I went into the bathroom and flicked on the light. I turned on the water to make it sound like I was washing my hands. Then I snuck across the hall into Justin's room. I found what I was looking for in his closet. A green hooded sweatshirt — with grease stains. The loose bike chain, of course! It was all the proof I needed.

Now I had to confront Justin. I went back and challenged him to a wrestling match. "Nah, too busy," Justin replied, staring at the TV.

"Chicken," I said, flapping my arms like wings. "*Bawk-ba-bawk.*"

That did it. Ten seconds later, we were out on the front lawn. Mila and Ralphie followed us out. Justin put my head into a hammerlock. *Wham!* He flung me to the ground.

I whispered into his ear. *"I know you stole it."*

Justin's eyes narrowed. He tightened the hammerlock.

"Don't say another word," he threatened. "Or you'll ruin everything."

I wasn't exactly having a wonderful time. Hammerlocks have that effect on me.

Justin leaned close to me. "You don't understand," he hissed through gritted teeth. "Trust me."

I did what I had to do.

"Confess!" I screamed. "Tell Ralphie the TRUTH!"

Chapter Twelve

Big Blue

"Tell me what?" Ralphie asked. "What are you blabbering about, Jigsaw?"

Justin stood up. He glared down at me. I didn't care. I was too busy fumbling around on the ground, making sure my head was still attached to my body.

Justin held up five fingers. "Give me five minutes. First I have to make a phone call." He stormed inside the house.

"What's going on?" Ralphie asked.

"Just wait," I said, rubbing my neck.

A minute later, Justin wheeled down the driveway on his skateboard. "I'll be right back," he shouted. "Jigsaw, don't say another word."

Poor Ralphie looked totally confused. He asked, "What's going on, guys?"

"*Mmmmmmrrrrrffff, mmmmmrrrrfffff,*" I mumbled.

"He can't talk," Mila observed.

Five minutes came and went. Ten minutes. Fifteen. Finally, Justin rode up on a sparkling blue bicycle. It had a new seat, new handlebars, new pedals. The spokes were shiny and clean.

Even the paint was dry.

Justin climbed off the bike and handed it to Ralphie. "Here," he said. "Call it an early birthday present." Justin glanced at me and smirked. He didn't seem angry.

Ralphie's jaw dropped open. "A new bike? For me?"

"Look closer, little brother. It's Old Rusty — new and improved. I paid someone to fix it up."

My eardrums almost burst from Ralphie's wild, joyous screams.

Justin explained everything. "I wanted to surprise you," he told Ralphie. "I thought it would be cool if you thought it was stolen. That would make you even happier when you got Old Rusty back."

Ralphie finally understood. "*You* stole Old Rusty?!" he said, disbelieving.

Justin nodded toward Mila and me. "Ask the detectives," he said. "They have it all figured out."

Ralphie gazed happily at Old Rusty. "It was a rotten trick," he told Justin. "Worse than the phony ghost."

Justin smiled. "Maybe. But you *loved* the ghost trick. Admit it. I make life more interesting for you guys. Besides, aren't you happy now?"

Ralphie smiled wide. "Thanks — thanks a whole lot. You're the best big brother I've got."

"I'm the *only* big brother you've got, pal," Justin said with a laugh.

"Hold on," Mila said to Justin. "Jigsaw saw the Snarkster pay *you*. How do you explain that?"

"Pay me?" Justin asked. He shot me a look.

"I spied on you," I confessed. "In Snarky's garage."

Justin smiled. "You've got guts, Jigsaw. I have to give you credit. But I'm the one who paid Snarky. Maybe you saw him give me eight dollars change." He reached into his pocket and pulled out a five and three one-dollar bills.

Ralphie snatched the money from Justin's hands. He handed it to me.

"Hey!" Justin complained.

"Hay is for horses," Ralphie said. "But this money is for Jigsaw and Mila. They earned it."

Justin's face slowly broke into a smile.

"You're right, Ralphie. I guess maybe it was a nasty trick after all. Do you forgive me?"

"Forgive you?" Ralphie said. "This is one of the happiest days of my life!"

He gave his brother a high-five.

The case of the bicycle bandit was solved. Ralphie was smiling again. He had Old Rusty back, which he now called "Big Blue." And it turned out that he had a pretty terrific brother after all.

I whispered something to Mila. She smiled. "Great idea, Jigsaw."

So I waved the eight dollars in the air. "Let's celebrate with ice cream," I said. "It's our treat!"